Eagles

D1313411

Geoffrey Hudswell

DEDICATION

For Bente, without whose guidance and support I could not have written this book

CHARACTERS

Archie Pegg, the main man

Pegg's Family and Friends
Angie Mason Pegg's stepdaughter, Ross Mason Angie's husband, Catherine Rose Mason their daughter, Pat Warrington Pegg's partner and lover, Afrim Babic an entrepreneur, Fred the poodle

Pegg's Colleagues
Police Sergeant Janie Bellman Constable Terri Wilder Constable Greg Knight, Constable Matthew Boggis, Constable Melanie Hobson

The Good Guys
Mohammed (Mo) Shaqaz an Iranian refugee, Esi Nzema a solicitor Mo's partner, Darius and Muna Shaqaz Mo's parents, Tom O'Brien Major USAF
Chaim Eban lecturer in renewable energy Mossad agent,
Leila Hosein sales assistant Fashion Trends, Michael Ali sales assistant Fashion Trends

The Bad Guys
Mehran Pejman, Chief of Guardians (IRGC) in Mo's hometown back in Iran
Akbar Mashrani director of Fashion Trends, an undercover
Colonel IRGC Quds Force
Ali Mochta Ghazi Agricultural Attaché Iranian Embassy undercover Major IRGC Quds Force

Yusef-al-Haddad leader of Hezbollah militia fighters, Ahmad-bin-Khoury militia fighter, Kaled Harari militia fighter   Naji-bin-Azzi militia fighter

AUTHOR'S NOTE

This story is entirely a work of fiction. There were several military airfields in Norfolk. But with the exception of one, they have all closed. The United States Air Force base at North Wendlesham does not and never has, existed. All the other places mentioned, with exception of North Wendlesham, do exist.

The USAF units, 100th Fighter Wing and 60 Fighter Squadron are my invention. There was a 100th Fighter Wing but it was disbanded 7 November 1945, likewise the 60th Fighter Squadron was disbanded on 1 January 2009.

This novel follows on from *A Veteran's Quest for Justice*, which introduced Archie Pegg.

ACKNOWLEDGMENTS

I am a person who does not have the resources to travel around the globe in order to carry out research for the material to write a book. I am therefore grateful being able to access Wikipedia. This wonderful tool is a treasure trove of facts and figures. Long may we be able to benefit from its fountain of knowledge.

I would also like to extend my sincere thanks to all those friends and family who have encouraged me in my second literary endeavour.

The Norfolk and Norwich Hospital is one of three general hospitals in Norfolk. I have the greatest admiration for the work this establishment does. Two major characters have their lives saved as a result of the skills and devotion of the staff. It is my view that the care which the patients in the book received, would be a fact of life in the real world. I hope that this book will go a little way to show how much I admire our National Health Service.

ABOUT THE AUTHOR

Geoffrey Hudswell was born in Cromer, Norfolk 74 years ago. As well as working in the United Kingdom, he has lived and worked in Norway and Germany. He was educated at Worksop College in Nottinghamshire. After leaving school he enlisted in the army - first into the 17/21 Lancers and on transfer, he served in the Royal Engineers. He had a four year break in army service before re-enlisting into the Royal Engineers, completing 23 years' service. He retired in 1990 and left the Sappers in the rank of warrant officer. Geoffrey joined the Norfolk Constabulary and served with the police until the mandatory retirement age of 55. He went on to work in the insurance industry, both as a claims investigator and as a loss adjuster. He retired at the age of 70. "Guardians and Eagles" is his second novel.

"For their heart studieth destruction, and
their lips talk of mischief".
Proverbs Chapter 24 verse 2

CHAPTER 1

Mohammed Shaqaz was an Iranian, he arrived in England as an asylum seeker. Since his arrival in the country, he was determined to make a life for himself, and try and give something back to the land which had given him a safe haven. He had been forced to leave his native Iran. He was not a threat to the Islamic Republic, neither was he a terrorist, fighting to bring down the Ayatollahs' Theocracy. The only "crime", Mohammed, or Mo as he was known, had committed was in his sexual orientation; he was gay. His lover back in Iran had been murdered by members of Sepah-e-Pasdaran or The Army of the Guardians of the Islamic Republic known in the rest of the world as the Iranian Revolutionary Guards Corps (IRGC). Mo's family had assisted him to flee the country. As a result of this, his parents, Darius and Muna Shaqaz, had attracted the attention of some of the vindictive elements of the Guardians. These evil people were making the lives of Darius and Muna as difficult as possible. They were both teachers, but the malevolence of the Guardians led to them both losing their jobs. They had to take on employment as low paid cleaners. The severe decrease in their incomes meant that they were living in abject poverty.

Mo and his lover had run a clothing business, which had thrived even in the harsh economic climate at the time of sanctions against the Islamic Republic. It was perhaps because of this, that Mo and his lover came to the attention of the local Guardians' commander, Mehran Pejman. Pejman was an ambitious and corrupt man, enriching himself at the regime's expense. His nefarious activities reached into every part of his area of control and beyond, treating it as his own fiefdom. His superiors either had no knowledge of his activities, or they chose to ignore them. Pejman wanted Mo's business for himself. He

1

offered a paltry sum to buy Mo and his lover out. The young men refused to have anything to do with the offer. They had worked hard to build the business up, and no corrupt official was going to take it away from them. They were blissfully unaware of the vindictive nature of the local Guardian commander, Mehran Pejman.

Nothing more happened until a few weeks later. Mo had been visiting his parents and was away from the apartment he shared with his lover. When he returned, he entered the entrance lobby and was about to ascend the stairs to get to his flat. He stopped when a woman who lived on the ground floor, came out of her apartment and beckoned him. He went towards her, she grabbed hold of his arm and pulled him into her apartment, once he was inside, she went to the doorway and looked out to see if anyone was about, after which she closed the door. The woman looked terrified, and there were tears streaming down her face.

She explained that a group of men, five in number and dressed in black, had entered the apartment block and gone upstairs to Mo's apartment, which happened to be above hers. She heard a disturbance, screaming and shouting, and what sounded like furniture thrown being thrown about., then it went quiet. She started sobbing as she went on to describe how about thirty minutes later this group of men came down the stairs to the entrance lobby. They were laughing and shouting, and she saw that two of them were carrying something in a rolled-up carpet. She was standing in the doorway of her flat. She recognised one of the men as being one of the local Guardians. The man came over to her and told her if she said anything about what she had seen he would kill her. She urged Mo not to go to his flat, she hugged him and begged him to leave immediately. Mo fled the scene and contacted his parents. Darius told Mo that people had visited the house looking for him. They were from the so called "Morality Police". These fanatics stated that they wanted Mo for offences against public decency, a euphemism for homosexuality.

The following day an old friend of Darius drove Mo over the border into Pakistan, where he was smuggled aboard a freighter docked in the port of Karachi. Once aboard the ship's master, who had been paid handsomely, put Mo to work as a steward-cum-cook's assistant. Two weeks later the boat docked in Sherness, where Mo applied for asylum. His application was eventually processed, and he was granted permanent residence in the United Kingdom. This was important as it meant that he was able to work. He had not wasted his time whilst he was waiting for his application for asylum to be granted. He studied English and became proficient at both reading and writing, and of course, speaking the language. He read about adoptive country and its history. By the time he was granted permanent residence he was in a good position to take up employment. He eventually got a job working in a ladies' and gentlemen's outfitters.

He worked hard and was extremely popular with the clientele. It was not long before he was offered an assistant manager's post at the company's branch in Norwich. In the meantime, he studied in the evenings and obtained a Business Diploma. He managed to save a fair amount of money, and when the chance came up for him to start up on his own, he took it. In Dereham, which was a market town about fifteen miles to the west of Norwich, he had found a run-down shop which had two floors. The shop had closed down some time ago, and the commercial property agents, had not found anyone interested in taking up the leasehold. The shop was near to the town centre. A lot of work was required for the premises to be brought up to the standard Mo wanted.

There were some generous grants available, and no business rates to pay for eighteen months. The leasehold was up for sale, there was a possibility of eventually buying the freehold. What was there not to like? Mo's bankers examined his business plans. A business loan and mortgage were approved.

Mo had by this time been in a new relationship. His partner was an older man of Ghanaian heritage, Esi Nzema. Esi was a solicitor, specializing in criminal law. He was employed by a firm located in Norwich, where he was head of the firm's criminal law department. He was very good at his job. Police officers knew that if Esi was the defence solicitor in any magistrate court proceedings, he would be a formidable opponent. All cases had to be watertight, any small loose end and Esi would be sure to find it and exploit it for all it was worth.

Police officers regarded him as an honourable man, who, as a hard-working advocate, strived to do the best for his clients. It was no surprise that the Norfolk Police Federation always instructed him when members needed a solicitor to represent them. He had a particularly good track record in getting claims made against police officers thrown out. Mo and Esi lived in a large detached house about a mile to the west of the city centre of Norwich.

Mo's new business started trading in early January of 2015, under the name Elite Clothing. As with the previous enterprises that Mo had been involved with, the business thrived. The shop sold ladies and gentlemen's fashions, stocking well-known brands. Both town and country styles could be found in store. The shop also sold footwear. He also rented out storage space on one of the town's industrial estates, which he utilized as a warehouse. Mo had applied for British citizenship, and in March the same year, he was granted it.

His prosperity enabled him to remit increasing sums of money to his desperate parents back in Iran. These remittances did much to alleviate much of the poverty they had to endure after Mo's sudden departure. These additional funds enabled his ailing father to obtain much

4

needed medical treatment. They were able to replace the monies they had spent in getting Mo to safety. Mo would have dearly loved to have them join him in the UK, but in spite of the attention they were getting from Mehran Pejman, Iran was their home and they felt they were too old to make the changes.

Mo was immensely popular with his customers, one of whom was Archie Pegg. He was developing into "pillar of the community". He sponsored a local women's netball team as well as a host of local charities. He declined the opportunity to become involved in local politics, despite many invitations by agents of the local Labour, Liberal Democrat and Conservative parties.

However, Dark forces were at work which would seriously affect Mo's ambitions for the future.

CHAPTER 2

Police Sergeant Archie Pegg was the Patrol Sergeant in charge of B Relief at Dereham Police Station. In order to enable the policing of this part of central Norfolk to be covered, staffing was organised such that there were five constables operating out of Dereham, and a further three working from Swaffham.

Pegg was formerly a staff sergeant in the Royal Engineers. He had served in a number of operational theatres, including Northern Ireland during "the Troubles", the Balkans, the First Iraq War and the Falkland Islands. He had been a police officer for 15 years, and at the age of fifty five he could have retired, but he had decided to continue. He was a widower; his wife Cath had been killed in a car crash. Her car had been in a collision with a vehicle that was being driven by a drunk driver. The man involved was jailed for six years. He would be out of prison in thirty months, having served half his sentence. It was a situation which Pegg found difficult to come to terms with. He was close to his stepdaughter, Angie Mason, Cath's daughter, and of course Angie's daughter Catherine Rose. Pegg had no children of his own.

Pegg was currently on night shift. He had been out on foot patrol with a Special Constable in the town. The Special was due to finish at two o'clock that morning, he had started at nine the previous evening. He had volunteered to stay on as it had been a busy Friday night.   There had been a number of incidents in Dereham, and in addition, there had been some trouble in one of the villages in the Swaffham area. The result of all this disorder was there were five young men in custody, all of whom would be charged with public order offences when they sobered up.

It was about three o'clock, when Pegg heard on the radio that one of the Swaffham cars had come across a single vehicle collision on the Fakenham to North Wendlesham road. There appeared to be four injured, two adults and two small children. The two adults were in a bad way. A supervisor will be required at the scene. There were no traffic officers available as there had been multiple collisions on the A47, some of them were fatal. The weather had been wet and although the rain had stopped, the temperature had dropped to below zero, now there was a danger of black ice on road surfaces.

Pegg informed the control room that he was en route to the incident. The Special offered to go with him. Pegg did not know what the situation on the ground was, so he was grateful for any help. Fifteen minutes later Pegg arrived at the scene of the incident. A police car was already there Parked diagonally across the road with its strobe beacons flashing. A BMW 3 series saloon car was lying on its roof in a ditch, having come to rest in front of a large oak tree. The impact had crushed the front end of the car. The collision had occurred on a bend. There were two officers at the stricken vehicle, one was lying on her front trying to communicate with the occupants, the other was tugging frantically at the rear door. Pegg spoke to the officer tugging at the door:

"Okay, Matt what have we got here, and what have you done so far?"

"Fire and ambulance are en route, a first responder is coming out of Fakenham, this may be the first medic on scene. All the rest of the resources are tied up on the A47 with the multiple fatal RTC's. I do not know how long it will be before we get any help. I cannot get the door open and Mel says it's reeking with petrol in the car."

"It's okay son, you've done well. Let's get the doors open in case the whole thing brews up." He shouted at the Special:

"Get the wrecking bar out of the back of our car now!" "It's not good sarge," said Pc Matthew Boggis, "I don't think the two adults in the front are going to make it." Pegg squatted down beside Pc Melanie Hobson, she was speaking to two small children about two years old, strapped in two child seats. The children were upside down, and Pegg could see that petrol was dripping onto their small bodies. They were both crying. The seats had at least preventing them from any major injuries.

The Special had the wrecking bar, and was proceeding to jimmy the back door open, he passed a seat belt cutter to Pegg. Mel meanwhile had managed to reach through the broken driver's window and turned off the ignition. The door was forced open, and Pegg reached inside and cut the nearest tot, a boy, free from the seat belt holding his child seat in position. He passed him out to Mel, he repeated the operation with the other child, a girl, and passed her out to the Special.

Pegg looked into the front of the car. He had seen enough trauma in his life to know that the driver and his passenger were beyond help. The car was a left-hand drive model, the driver was a man in his mid-twenties, he was trapped by his legs, and the steering wheel was embedded in his chest, his eyes were open, felt his neck, there was no pulse. He looked across to the front seat passenger, a woman, about the same age as the driver, judging by the position of her head, it was clear to Pegg her neck was broken, reached across and took he wrist; there was no pulse.

"Don't attempt to take those kids out of their child seats, wait for the medics, get some blankets and keep them warm. Stay clear of the car. We don't know if the fuel is going to up."

"Looks like the medics are here." said Boggis.

Pegg got up from the crashed car and could see a vehicle pull up, its blue lights were flashing. It was the First Responder's estate. The medic got out and went over to the crashed car. Pegg briefed him. He went to the driver's side and crouched down and reached inside. A few moments later he withdrew his arms. He looked at Pegg and shook his head. He went to his car and came back with a bag. Pegg took him to where the children were. The medic examined each one in turn.

"These two mites appear not to have any broken bones, a few cuts and grazes, but apart from reeking of petrol, there's not much physically wrong with them. They'll need a thorough check in hospital. Any idea what their names are?" he said.

"Not yet," replied Pegg, "as soon as we can get the other two out of the car, we can have a look for some form of ID. We'll have to wait for the Fire to get them out, and make sure the car is safe. There's petrol leaking out all over the place, it's even got onto the little ones."

An ambulance arrived, shortly followed by a fire appliance. The paramedic confirmed that the two adults were dead. The firefighter in charge of the appliance was informed. He and his crew proceeded to ensure that the crashed vehicle would not catch fire. They then started the sad task of extricating the dead occupants from the car. In the meantime, the ambulance took the two small children to hospital It was a cold night and the sooner they were in the warm the better.

The control room was informed that an undertaker's vehicle was required to take the bodies to the mortuary. Pegg waited for the firefighters to finish their task. The bodies were laid out next to the verge. Pegg searched the driver's body, whilst Hobson searched that of the passenger. The firefighters had also taken items from the car. There were some items of luggage, some toys, and a lady's handbag. These things were placed beside the bodies.

Pegg had found a wallet and a mobile phone on the dead male. He examined it and found a United States Air Force identity card in the name of Mario Posetti, cash, both sterling and dollars, and an air force driving permit, in the name of Staff Sergeant Mario Posetti. The handbag, which Hobson had searched had yielded a USAF family identity card in the name of Lucia Posetti. There was also a photograph in a purse, of a young man holding a small child in each of his arms. On the back of the picture was written, "Mario and our twins Gino and Guilia."

It was getting on for half past five. Pegg asked Hobson to take his car and drive the Special and the Posetti's belongings back to Dereham and leave the stuff in the sergeants office. He had retrieved a camera from the car before they left. He updated the control room, regarding the two fatalities and the possible identities of the car's occupants. He requested the attendance of a traffic police Collision Investigator (CI). He was informed that there would be no CI available before mid-morning. Pegg said that he was still waiting for the undertakers to collect the bodies and convey them to the mortuary. The control room told Pegg to process the scene as best he could.

Pegg, assisted by Boggis, took photographs and measurements. Once this was done, he completed a Road Traffic Collision booklet, as far as he could. He then

10

took photographs of the two bodies as they lay on their backs, and close ups of their faces. After closing their eyes, he took a further photograph of each face.

The undertaker's ambulance arrived. It was a bit of a misnomer to call it a vehicle an ambulance, it was a large Transit size panel van, with removable gurneys to transport dead bodies, either to a hospital's mortuary, or to the undertaker's premises. The two men who exited the vehicle were soberly dressed in black overcoats, both were wearing white shirts and black ties. Their company was one of a number of such firms who were contracted out to HM
Coroner's Office.

The men came over and spoke with Pegg. They asked if the bodies had been searched. After being informed that this was the case, the undertakers returned to their vehicle and unloaded a gurney from the back and wheeled it over to Lucia's body. They placed it in a body bag, and lifted it onto the gurney, and wheeled it back to the van, loading it up. They repeated the process with Mario's body. Pegg was informed that they would be taken to the Norfolk and Norwich Hospital's mortuary.

When the undertakers had departed, Pegg and Boggis started the process of "marking off" the scene. The control room informed Pegg that the scene should be protected until a CI could attend and examine both the BMW and the immediate area of the collision. In Pegg's view there was no need to block off the road, he advised the control room of this. The controller concurred, with the caveat that the carriageway may have to be partially closed off for the CI to carry out a more detailed examination.

Pc Hobson arrived back with Pegg's car. She said that the Special had made a statement before signing off and left it in Pegg's pigeonhole. She'd left the recovered items and luggage in the temporary property store.

It was getting on for seven o'clock. Pegg told Boggis and Hobson to remain at the scene; and after ensuring that the control room would arrange for them to be relieved when the day shift reported on for duty, drove back to Dereham police station.

When he got back he obtained the details of the CI who would be attending the scene. Once he had the information he uploaded the photos he had taken and with the scanned pages of the collision booklet, emailed them to the CI. He also left a message on the officer's voicemail. He then called the main telephone switch board at RAF North Wendlesham. A female voice answered the call, she spoke with a soft American accent:

"Switchboard RAF North Wendlesham, how may we help you sir"

"This is sergeant Pegg, Dereham police, I need to speak to the station duty officer. It's urgent."

"What is the nature of your enquiry with the duty officer sir?"

"There's no easy way of telling you this, but it concerns a fatal traffic collision involving one of your airmen and his family."

There was a long pause before the call taker replied in a very subdued tone:

"Putting you through now sir."

Pegg heard a few clicks followed by a dialling tone. The phone was picked up:

"Captain Gomez."

Pegg introduced himself and the reason he was calling.

"Do you have the names of the folks who were involved?"

"Staff Sergeant Mario Posetti, and a woman called Lucia Posetti, these details were obtained from documents found on the bodies of the deceased. There were two small children in the vehicle as well. They are alive and are currently at the Norfolk and Norwich Hospital under observation, their injuries appear to be minor." The captain said nothing.

"Hello, are you still there sir?"

"Yes, I'm sorry sergeant. I'm trying to take it all in. Go on."

"Is Mario Posetti one of yours?"

"Yes, he is. He is an armourer with 60 Fighter Squadron, he and his family live on base in the married quarters. Okay let me take some details from you sergeant Pegg."

Pegg spent the next ten minutes informing Captain Gomez where the children and the bodies of their parents had been taken to. He said that incident was being investigated by Road Policing department, the vehicle involved was yet to be examined by police, so at this stage the cause of the collision could not be verified. Property from the vehicle had been recovered and was currently at Dereham Police station. He concluded the call by leaving his contact details. He said he would let the day shift sergeant know about the incident. If he needed to be contacted, Pegg would next be on duty at eleven o'clock that evening. He informed Gomez that the deceased persons' phones would be retained for evidential purposes, and for examination by the CI.

Next, Pegg contacted the officers who had assisted at the scene, he had the private mobile numbers of both Hobson and Boggis. He asked each in turn how they were feeling, they were both a bit down, but they were bearing up. Pegg told them to contact him at any time if they wanted to talk about it. He gave them his mobile and home phone numbers. Next, he looked up the Special's contact details. He decided to send him an email rather than phone, as he was probably in bed. The contents of the email reflected the phone conversations he just had with Boggis and Hobson. It was already past nine o'clock when Pegg drove out of the police station, He went home and straight to bed.

CHAPTER 3

At RAF North Wendlesham, Major Tom O'Brien of the United States Air Force was being briefed by the air base's duty officer Captain Manual Gomez.

RAF North Wendlesham is a large United States Air Force base located a few miles from Dereham. The USAF, (it had previously been part of the US Army, known as the USAAF), had taken over the airfield officially in 1948, at the start of the cold war. Although US aircraft had been operating from there in 1942, the air station was closed in 1945, and put on a care and maintenance footing by the Air Ministry. At the start of the Berlin Airlift in June 1948 units of the newly formed USAF, (it became independent of the US Army in 1947), started to operate out of the airfield. When the Airlift finished in May 1949, the USAF moved in on a permanent basis.

Over the years the USAF had operated several types of aircraft from the air base. The Boeing B29 Superfortress and its upgraded version the B-50D, the B-47, and later the F111. The McDonnell Douglas F15 Strike Eagle is the type of aircraft currently operating out the air base. It was used as a multi role fighter. There were four Squadrons of this type of aircraft permanently stationed there. US Air National Guard and US Air Force Reserve units temporarily operated out of the airbase as well.

Major O'Brien was the current Deputy Commander of the 60th Fighter Squadron, one of four making up the 100th Fighter Wing. He was a slim man of Irish American stock whose family were from Boston, Massachusetts. He was forty-five and had been an airman since the age of eighteen. His family were quite poor, but despite this he had grown up in a loving environment. He enlisted in the air force as an airman, and he was eventually selected for officer training. After attendance at the USAF Officer Training School in Colorado, he attended the air force's flight school at Vance AFB in Oklahoma and qualified as a fast jet pilot.

He was deeply saddened by the loss of one of his airmen, especially Mario Posetti. Mario in a way was very much like O'Brien in that he also came from a poor background. Mario had made the air force his life. He had earned his stripes, and he was shortly due to be promoted to Technical Sergeant, or "Tech Five" as it was colloquially known in the USAF, due to the five bar chevrons which marked these NCOs' badge of rank. O'Brien had even talked to Mario regarding becoming a commissioned officer, and to that end the young airman had been studying to get the academic qualifications.

"Fucking waste, Manuel! Two great young people dead, two kids orphaned. Right let's get to it. What have we got so far? Where are the parents and where are the kids now?"

"Sir, the local police have had the bodies of Staff Sergeant and Mrs Posetti taken to the mortuary of the Norfolk and Norwich Hospital, the kids were taken to the Accident and Emergency section of the same hospital."

"Who is the police officer dealing with this?"

"A sergeant Pegg, who is based at Dereham, sir."

"Have you got his contact details?"

Gomez gave him a sheet of paper on which he'd written not only Pegg's telephone numbers, but also his email address. In addition, he written a brief report about the incident as he was given it by Pegg. Pegg had also informed Gomez that although he was not on duty until eleven that evening, in view of the nature of the incident, please leave a message on his email. Pegg said that he monitors it regularly.

"Seems Sergeant Pegg is on night shifts, well I'll send him an email, and I'll try one of the phone numbers. Right what about next of kin?"

"It would appear in the light of what has happened, it seems that we need to only contact Mrs Posetti's parents, as Staff Sergeant Posetti's mom and dad are both dead, and we have no record of him having any siblings."

"Mario must have had nominated a next of kin."
"Lucia Posetti, Sir."

"Shit I forgot that Manuel."

"Has anyone been in contact with Lucia's parents?"

"That's in hand, the base records office is arranging for a local New York USAF officer and a padre to visit them."

"And the twins?"

"We're in touch with the hospital, we will arrange for them to be brought back to base, as soon as the Norwich hospital releases them." Gomez paused, he continued:

"Sir, there is the matter of identifying the bodies of the Posettis."

"It'll be me, it's the least I can do. I saw a lot of the family, I knew Mario from work as well, and Lucia, I met her on many occasions at Base parties and Squadron dos. Right Manuel keep me in the loop regarding the NOK. Leave the rest to me. I'm not due to do any flying before Tuesday, it's Saturday today, despite it being a weekend, we can get a lot done."

* * *

O'Brien left it until two o'clock that afternoon before he attempted to telephone Pegg, he'd already sent an email to the officer, using his police address. Pegg was woken by the sound of his official issue mobile's ringtone.

"Hello."

16

"Is that sergeant Pegg?"

"Speaking, who are you?" said Pegg drowsily. "I guess I've woken you up, I'm sorry about that, but I really need some info, I'm Major Tom O'Brien from RAF Wendlesham, I am told you are the officer dealing with the incident in which one of my airmen was killed along with his wife. I am Mario Posetti's Deputy Squadron Commander." Pegg sat up, and clearing his head he said:

"Right sir how can I help?"

"Well I want to know what the procedures regarding this whole unhappy episode are, especially regarding the kids."

"We, that is myself and my colleagues came across the car; it was upside down in a ditch. There appeared to be no other vehicle involved. The two people in front of the car had suffered traumatic injuries and were pronounced dead at the scene. The children were still strapped in their child seats, which was what probably saved them. But when we tried to extricate them from the vehicle, we found that the door was jammed. At first, we were unable to open the door. We were very concerned as to the danger the children were in. There appeared to be a fractured fuel line, and petrol was leaking into the car."

"Geez! So, what happened?"

Pegg went on to explain how he, Hobson and Boggis, managed to get the twins out. The twins were examined at the scene before being taken to the Norfolk and Norwich hospital. He went on to explain although he had taken measurements and completed a Collision Report, the whole scene would be examined by a specialist traffic officer, the CI, before the vehicle is recovered. Pegg informed O'Brien, the CI had in all probability attended, and finished his work. The car would have been taken to a secure compound for the CI to examine. Pegg continued:

"Sir, there are some issues you need to be aware of. HM Coroner in Norwich has jurisdiction regarding the investigation into the deaths of your airman and his wife. The Coroner's officer will be the interface. I know him quite well, and I will certainly intercede on your behalf. There is the matter of the formal identification the deceased persons."

"I can do that; I knew them both personally," said O'Brien.   "Once there has been a post-mortem examination, I am sure that the Coroner will authorize the release of their bodies to your organisation."

"My next question is regarding the kids. What will happen to them?"

"Well I should imagine that there would in normal cases if the children were from a local family, they would go to the nearest relatives, but in this case from what I presume the children's next of kin are not immediately available. So
Social Services could temporarily take over."
O'Brien said nothing.

"Hello, are you still on the line sir?" Pegg asked.

"I'm sorry sergeant, I am thinking. My wife June and I were pretty close to the family, the twins know her quite well, and they have been around to our house on many occasions. What if I said that we would take them in until a permanent arrangement can be made for them?"

"That seems to be an ideal solution. I'll contact the hospital and let you know when the kids will be fit to be discharged."

They spoke for a few more minutes, before Pegg ended the call. Pegg got showered and dressed. He phoned the hospital and was put through to the paediatric ward. He spoke to the ward sister. The children were ready to be discharged, but in view of their parents being killed, where

18

would they go to. Pegg explained the circumstances regarding the children's background. He said that Tom and June O'Brien would care for the children until they could be re-united with immediate family in the US.

The sister appeared relieved to hear this news. She took the contact details for the O'Briens. Pegg asked how the twins were bearing up. She told him that in view of what they had been through, they were in surprisingly good shape. But the best place for them would be a home environment and not a hospital ward. Next, he called the Pathology Department and asked to be put through to the mortuary. He spoke to a member of staff. As a result of this conversation, a formal identification of the Posetti's bodies was arranged for 10:30 on Sunday morning. Post-mortems were arranged to start at ten on Monday morning. The Coroner's Officer would be present, and as a courtesy, because an American Serviceman and a Serviceman's dependent were the deceased, a Medical Officer from RAF North Wendlesham had been invited to attend as well.   Pegg spent the rest of the day relaxing, before going back to bed again. He slept for four hours before waking up at nine. By a quarter to ten he was back behind his desk in Dereham station's Sergeants' Office. After briefing the night shift officers, he went to see the inspector. He wanted to recommend Hobson, Boggis and the Special for a" Good

Police Work" award, for their part in rescuing the Posetti twins. The inspector read through Pegg's recommendation report and endorsed it. The report would go up to the Superintendent for approval.

Saturday and Sunday's night shifts went without any major incident, and by Monday morning Pegg was back home, having been re-united with his devoted companion, his black poodle dog, Fred. Whilst Pegg had been on nights, Angie Ross, his stepdaughter had been looking after him. Now Pegg was a sergeant it was difficult to have Fred at work. It had been an open secret that Pegg always had the animal with him on nights when he was a rural beat officer. After collecting Fred from Angie's, Pegg returned Gressenhall, and parked up.

He collected some shears, secateurs, and a bunch of flowers. After placing the items in a bag, he took Fred for a walk. Their immediate destination was the church of St Mary the Virgin, Gressenhall. They walked past the Green, and south down Church Lane, and into the churchyard. He went to Cath's grave, and after tidying up, he replaced the flowers in the vase. He decided to stick to carnations and chrysanthemums, as these did not seem to be eaten by the ubiquitous rabbits. When he had finished, he sat down on the small folding stool, he'd brought with him. Fred sat next to him, he whined:

"I know we all miss her."

Pegg remained there for a further fifteen minutes, before he gathered his things together and took the long way back to the house.

CHAPTER 4

The Iranian Revolutionary Guards Corps is known in Iran as Sepeh-e-Pasdaran, or the Army of Guardians. It was founded in 1979 by order of Ayatollah Rubollah Khomeini.

Its mission was to defend the Revolution after the fall of the Shah. The force is currently 125,000 strong, which is augmented by the Basij militias, whose active membership is 90,000. The Army of Guardians as an organisation has its own land, sea, and air arms. In addition, there is the Quds (Jerusalem) Force.

This is the specialist and elite section of the Army of Guardians or the Iranian Revolutionary Guards Corps (IRGC) as it is referred to internationally. The Quds Force supports operations outside the Islamic Republic. It has its tentacles in many areas, supporting and training militias such as Hezbollah in Lebanon, Hamas in Gaza and the West Bank, Shia militias in Iraq and Syria, plus covert operations elsewhere outside the borders of Iran.   In Iran, the local IRGC commander, Mehran Pejman, an ambitious man, has a plan which will possibly help him climb up the hierarchy of the organisation. He put his idea to the Guardians provincial command. They listened to his plans. They said that the project was a good idea and agreed with him; there were some caveats. They would not give him any official backing; Tehran and the Islamic Republic's government would be in the dark and would know nothing of the plan. He would have to use his own resources to get the project going and in achieving its goal.   If it was successful, then he would be given full credit for it. But even so the Islamic Republic, could not admit any responsibility.

However, should it fail, then any repercussions would be on his head. These were odds that the Pejman was prepared to accept, as he knew success would take him to the top of the organisation. What the provincial command or the upper echelons of the Guardians did not know, was that Pejman, along with a small group Guardians officers, were aiming to take over the organisation and pursue even more radical goals, than the current leadership of the organisation.

He started by contacting a "fixer" in Syria. The means of communication was a satellite phone. The fixer was involved in several criminal activities; drug and people smuggling, money laundering, arms dealing and slavery.

Like all successful fixers the man never got involved directly in these distasteful enterprises. He did not care who his clients were or what they represented, as long as he was paid for his services.

Pejman gave the fixer a list of his requirements. The price was agreed. The money coming from Pejman's own substantial financial resources. He had a fortune in offshore accounts, money earned from nefarious activities of his own, money which his superiors had no knowledge of. He was in a hurry to move on. He had already committed enough offences to merit his execution many times over. He'd got away with it so far, there was no reason for that to change any time soon. The price to be paid was half now, and the rest on the successful delivery of all the ordered items and the training of personnel. An hour later the fixer contacted Pejman to inform half of the agreed sum was already in the offshore account, the details of which the fixer had given.

Pejman had Mo's parents under close but discreet surveillance ever since Mo had fled the country. He had arranged for the disposal of the body of Mo's murdered lover. It was lying somewhere on the bottom of the Gulf of Iran. The clothing shop he had stolen from Mo was doing reasonably well, not as well as when Mo had it, but not too badly given the precarious state of the country's economy.

* * *

As a result of the fixer's endeavours an articulated pantechnicon drove over the border with Turkey and into Bulgaria. The vehicle was loaded with domestic appliances, electric cookers, refrigerators, and freezers. The cargo was genuine, and the only thing that the customs at the Bulgarian frontier were checking, was for illegal immigrants and drugs. In the case of the pantechnicon, as additional security, corrupt customs officials were handsomely remunerated in order that not too much attention was paid to the pantechnicon's cargo.

After a brief cursory check, the pantechnicon was waved through. It continued its journey through mainland Europe until it reached the port at Hoek van Holland, in the Netherlands. There it drove onto a RORO ferry for the crossing to Harwich.

On arrival in Harwich the pantechnicon quickly cleared the checks at the port and was on its way to a goods depot in Chelmsford, where its load of appliances was offloaded. The appliances were arranged ready for collection by various wholesaler customers. Two dozen of the boxed appliances were collected and loaded onto a white 5 tonne DAF Luton van and driven to small industrial estate at the edge of Reydon near the seaside town of Southwold in Suffolk. There the van was parked up in a unit which had been rented on a temporary basis.

The van's load was removed, and the appliances were unpacked. The load had consisted entirely of twenty-four cardboard crates labelled as freezers, both chest and upright. The only resemblance these items had with the original state when they had left the factory in Turkey, was their external appearance Somewhere between their journey from factory to the Bulgarian border, the freezers workings had been stripped out and repacked with the items the fixer in Syria had supplied, and loaded on again with the genuine unadulterated articles.

The contents of the twenty-four freezer carcasses were removed and repacked into another set of cardboard crates, this time sixteen in number, which were labelled as clothing. Once done the carcasses were loaded onto the van again. The unit was secured, and the van drove to London with its disembowelled freezers. Some weeks later the same van collected the repacked cardboard crates, this time it drove north to the east Midlands, its final destination being a small industrial estate on the northern edge of Nottingham.

The first part of Mehran Pejman's plan had been achieved. The next part of the plan was to contact a

Lebanese Militia group which often acted as surrogates for the IRGC Quds Force. Members of this militia had agents working throughout Europe. The agents facilitated the training of an elite section of the militia. They were well versed in using the equipment that the fixer had supplied, and for which Pejman had paid him handsomely.

CHAPTER 5

Mo Shaqaz was already in his clothing shop, the enterprise opened at nine o'clock, but Mo was there at eight. He was nearly always there before his staff arrived. He was also the last to leave after the shop closed at six o'clock. He had a deputy manager, a competent woman, who he could trust to run the business on those occasions when he was away on holiday or visiting suppliers. He had enough staff to ensure that in addition to Sundays, they had a day off in the week, to compensate for working on Saturdays, and of course holiday cover.

Monday mornings were generally quiet, which is why Mo was in his office sorting out some orders and phoning up the suppliers, confirming the orders he had already placed. The phone rang. It was one of the sales assistants calling from the ground floor sales desk.

"Excuse me Mr Shaqaz, but there is a gentleman downstairs, wanting to speak to you."

"Did he say who he was Susan?"

"He said it was a private matter."

"Okay, tell him to wait there and I'll send Amanda down to show him up."

Mo switched the monitor on his desktop to the CCTV camera which, covered the area of the ground floor sales desk. The man speaking to Susan was wearing a baseball cap and a hoodie, the lower part of his body was obscured by the counter. He got up and went to the door of his office:

Amanda" he called.

"Coming, Mr Saquaz."

A few seconds later Mrs Amanda Joyce came from her office. Amanda managed the accounts and filled in as Mo's secretary.

"Amanda there is a man downstairs with Susan can you show him up please."

She left and a few minutes later there was a knock on his office door.

"There's a Mr Ghazi here to see you."

"Show him in."

The visitor entered. He had removed his cap, and Mo could see the man had black close-cropped hair, and light brown eyes, he was quite tall about six feet, and of proportionate build. He spoke in Farsi:

"Salam va ashnai."

"Salam," replied Mo.

Mo continued the conversation in Farsi:

"Who are you and what do you want?"

"Your country needs your help."

"What are you talking about this is my country, the United Kingdom, England."

"No Mohammed Saquaz, Iran, the country of your birth."

"I have no ties with that land anymore, not since I was forced to flee, and my partner was brutally murdered. Now get out of here," he shouted.

Ghazi did not move, instead he took out an iPhone and tapped on its screen.

"I think you need to look at this video clip before you do anything else Mohammed," he said, showing the screen to Mo. Mo looked at the screen and gasped:

"Mama, Papa!"

"Yes, these images were taken yesterday. As you can see, they were on the way out to do some shopping. Your father is walking quite well thanks to the medication he is able to buy now, from the money which you send him each month."

"You bastards! What are you up to?" he yelled again.

"At the moment everything will carry on as normal, your parents will keep getting the money without any

26

interference, providing you give us a bit of help."   Mo's shouting had caused Amanda to knock on the door of the office.

"Is everything alright Mr Shaqaz, she asked through the closed door."

Mo got up and walked over to the door, opened it, and said to a worried looking Amanda Joyce:

"Everything is fine Amanda, just a little difference of opinion, just carry on with what you were doing, I'll be in in a minute to sign those invoices." He shut the door again, before continuing in English.

"I'll ask you again, what have you done with my parents?"   "Nothing has happened to them, as you can see the date on the video is yesterday, and nothing will happen to them."

"I can feel a big "but" coming."

"That is very astute of you Shaqaz, yes, there are a few "buts." We want you to do something for us. As long as you do as we ask, then as far as your parents are concerned, things will carry on as they are. They will continue to receive the money you send them, and your father will continue to be able to purchase the medication that he requires. I
expect that they know they are on our radar."

"Too right they do, your people have ensured Papa and Mama have lost their teaching jobs, they've lost their home. You're not dealing with confused elderly people here you know. If I am to be assistance to you, then I want something in return."

"You are not in a position to dictate terms Mr Shaqaz, but we are not unreasonable; maybe we can look again to see how things could be better for them," said Ghazi He gave Mo a folded piece of paper. "A phone number is written on this. You have 24 hours to come to a decision, call it if you have decided to help us. Oh, by the way, don't think of sharing anything I've told you." Ghazi left the office, saying, "I'll see myself out."

Mo looked at the piece of paper again. The number written on it appeared to be that of a mobile phone. He was in utter despair.

* * *

Ghazi returned to his car. He reached into the glove compartment and retrieved a satellite phone. He dialled a number.

"Well what news do you have for me?" a voice asked in Farsi.

"The message has been delivered and the recipient has been given a number to call, within 24 hours."

"Excellent my friend, we have achieved an important part of our plan. Does the Embassy know about your visit?"

"Don't worry they think I am in Norwich, which is where I'm going to next. If you need me for anything else, you know how to contact me."

The man called Ghazi ended the call. His full name was Ali Akbar Ghazi. He was actually an intelligence officer at the Iranian Embassy, but his official role was that of an Agricultural Attaché; but that was not all, he was in fact a major in the Al Quds Force, an elite branch of the IRGC. He was one of a small group of Guardians who were pursuing the same agenda as Pejman. He also wanted the organisation to adopt an even more radical stance both at home and abroad; to that end he was a willing accomplice of Pejman and his small group. After he had finished his telephone conversation. Ghazi drove to Norwich, where he was due to attend a symposium at the University of East Anglia's Earth Sciences Department, which was where the Embassy of the Islamic Republic believed him to be all the time.

CHAPTER 6

Pegg drove into Dereham, it was cold, windy and wet. He parked up in the Cowper Road car park. Fred looked out of the of the passenger window, and on seeing the rain coming down, looked at Pegg, sighed and settled down on his blanket, which was a permanent fixture on the seat.

"So, you're not interested in coming with me, boy?" The dog ignored him.

Pegg secured the Land Rover and walked towards the town centre. He looked in the window of Elite Clothing, there was a sale on and with offers on a variety of clothing. Pegg went in and started to browse amongst the menswear. He found a couple of sweatshirts, and a pair of cords. He went to the sales desk, and the assistant put the selected items aside, whilst Pegg went and looked at the Barbour clothing. Cath had been badgering him to replace the current jacket he had for years, and now it was practically falling apart. Pegg found a three-quarter length jacket which had a detachable lining, he looked at the price. It was quite dear, but in view of the brand's quality, it would last for years, and therefore worked out cheaper in the long run. He tried the jacket on. It was a good fit. He walked over to the sales desk and paid for the jacket and the other three items.

As the assistant packed and bagged up his purchases, he saw Amanda Joyce walking past, she was clearly distraught, her eyes were red, it was apparent that she had been crying. Pegg gathered up the bags and went over to her. She had been a close friend of Cath, and Pegg knew her quite well.

"Amanda, what on earth's happened?"

"Oh Archie, I don't know what to do," she said.

She took his arm and guided Pegg to a small alcove where some footwear was displayed, she looked round, before continuing,

"It's Mr Shaqaz, he's not like his usual self, he was going to sign off some invoices, he usually comes to my office and does it. When he failed to come in, I went to his office to remind him. I knocked and went in, and he shouted at me to get out and leave him alone, when I said it was important get the invoices signed, he got up, and slammed the door in my face. He said if I wanted to keep my job I should stay away."

"What do you suppose caused him to behave like he did?"

"Up to the point when he had this visitor, he was fine and his normal cheerful."

"What visitor was this, and when did this person arrive?"

"It was earlier this morning about an hour after we'd opened. This man, a foreigner I think, he looked like a southern European, maybe a Middle Easterner. This person asked to see Mr Shaqaz, about something important. I was asked by Mr Shaqaz to show him up.

'After I'd shown the man into his office. I closed the door. I couldn't help hearing that they were speaking in a foreign language. Any way I left to go back to my office to finish off some paperwork and get some invoices ready for signing off. I carried on working, when suddenly there was some shouting coming from Mr Shaqaz's office. I went to see if there was anything wrong, he told me not to worry, and shut the door in my face. About half an hour later the man left.'   'When Mr Shaqaz still hadn't come to sign of the invoices I went to his office, and he almost screamed at me to get out. I am so worried he's never been like this all the time I've known him."

"Don't worry, I'll pop up and have a word with him. I've got to know him quite well, and I've helped him with some crime prevention advice, so I think I've got I've got a foot in the door if you'll excuse the pun."

Pegg made his way up to Mo's office. He tapped on the door, "Mo," he said through the closed door."

"Go away, leave me be."

Pegg decided to grasp the nettle, he opened the door and went in. Before Mo could react Pegg put his forefinger to his lips, and said:

"Now don't start to shout the odds, we don't want the world and his wife listening in."

"Oh Mr Pegg, I'm sorry, but this is a very bad time."

"Archie please. I don't know what's upset you, but Amanda is in tears, and she is very concerned about you." Mo looked up from his desk, he looked dreadful. His hair was completely ruffled up, as if he had been scratching and running his hands through it. His tie was undone, and his face and eyes were reddened. He was sitting behind his desk, his head slumped on his elbows.

"There's nothing you can do Archie; it's best you leave me."

Pegg went around the desk and place a hand on Mo's right shoulder:

"Hey, hey, this isn't like you Mo, where's the brave young entrepreneur gone? Tell me what it is that's troubling you." Mo said nothing, he sat upright and gazed into space. "Come on speak to me, I'd like to think I'm a friend, a problem shared is a problem halved." Mo said nothing.

"Look is it to do with the guy who came to see you earlier?" Mo eventually said:,

"Archie you are a friend I know, but you are a policeman, you are the last person I should be speaking to."

"Look Mo, yes I'm a copper, but I've not got my policeman's head on at the moment, for a start, I'm on my rest days. So, anything we say, stays here, I mean it." Pegg was aware of Mo's circumstances in so far that he had been granted

31

asylum, and how he had worked hard to make a life for himself, but he was not aware of the events which led to him fleeing Iran.

"This morning I received a visitor who was, like me, an Iranian. Now you must promise me that what I tell you, does not leave this room; lives back in Iran are in grave danger. I am depending on you not to speak of what I am about to tell you."

Pegg agreed and gave Mo his word. Mo then told him about the visit and what the man called Ghazi had said. Pegg listened intently. He thought and said nothing for several minutes, and then he spoke:

"Right Mo, I will help you through this. We'll keep this to ourselves. But I've given you my word I'll speak to no one about this, but what I'm going to tell also stays between ourselves. I am going to do things which may cause me to lose my job, or even worse go to prison. But sometimes to get justice for people who mean a lot to me, I have to bend the rules so to speak."

"You can help with this without getting the police officially involved?"

"Yes, I've done it before, and we'll do it together. Your Mum and Dad will be okay. So, the first thing you are going to do, is to call that number this guy Ghazi gave you and say that you'll agree to help. I suggest you do it this evening, we want to give these people the impression you have thought long and hard before going through with it. Before I go, I'll take the number myself. I have ways of tracing it. It won't be legal, but nobody else will know that I'm doing it.
Do not tell anyone at all not even Esi."

Mo gave Pegg the piece of paper, that Ghazi had given to him. Pegg copied the number on a scrap of paper and put it in his wallet. They spoke for a few more minutes after which Pegg left. He collected his purchases from the sales desk on the ground floor and went out of the shop, and over to where he had left the Land Rover. He phoned Angie:

"Hi Archie, what gives?"

"Oh, you know, a couple of days off, and I'm at a bit of a loose end. I'd like to come over and see you all."

"Of course, come over and have a spot of lunch with us, Ross is away up in Scotland, Edinburgh, he'll be back tomorrow. We could do with a bit of company. Maybe we can take the baby out for a walk afterwards if it's not too wet."

"Sounds perfect, do you need me to pick something up for you on the way."

"No just bring yourself and the poodle, I take it he's with you?"

"Where else would he be! Be there in about twenty minutes."

Pegg drove out of Dereham and headed west along the A47 to Swaffham. A short while later he was parked outside Angie's house, a three-bedroom detached house just off the Brandon Road. He walked up the front path, Fred trotting beside him. Before he got to the front door, Angie had opened it, Fred went straight in without further ado. Pegg gave her a quick hug, and after closing the door behind him, followed her into the kitchen.

"Where's my little princess then?" Pegg had glanced into the living room and the playpen was empty. "I'm sorry Archie she was a bit grizzly and tired, teething and all that, she's upstairs asleep."

"Never mind it's probably for the best."

"Come on let's have something to eat, I've got some soup,
I made myself, and rolls, that okay?"

"Sounds good."

Angie heated up the soup. She laid out some bowls together with some rolls and butter. Pegg sat down. A few minutes later, she served the soup into bowls direct from the saucepan. She placed the bowls onto a tray and carried it over the table. They sat down and started on the soup. "So Archie, what are you going to do with your days off, are you going to see Pat, or is she coming down to yours?" She asked buttering a roll.

"As far as Pat is concerned, she may be coming down next weekend. Things have been a bit hectic at work for me; when is it never; so, I am trying to recharge my batteries before I return to the fray. But I have a bit of a problem, though" Pegg replied.

"Mmm, why am I getting a feeling that you want me to help you with something a bit dodgy?"

"Woman's intuition! There is something you could help me with, but if you don't want to, it matters not a lot" "So, you want me to use my skills and knowledge with something a bit moody?"

"If I give you a telephone number what can you tell me about it? Can you tell who the phone is registered to and stuff like that."

"I can do a lot more than that, I can hack into the provider and get the calls which have been made from it. I can get voicemail messages, as well as text messages. But, as you well know, it's all highly illegal."

"Well that's that then, I do not want to get you into any trouble."

"Archie, no! Don't you dare, you know jolly well I'll always assist you. I've helped you out before, it was for a noble cause, and I'm sure that this is for something in the same vein."

Angie Ross was a self-employed IT consultant. She worked mainly from home, and her work included checking and debugging companies' systems, and installing various apps to counter malware and cyberattacks. She was adept at hacking into emails and computer systems. She had helped Pegg previously. Pegg had been involved in trying to get justice for veterans who were wrongfully accused of

"war crimes" in the Balkans. It was a quest in which he was successful, and it resulted in the breaking up of a criminal ring which was submitting fictitious and fraudulent claims both against serving and retired members of the armed forces. Angie played no small part in the success of this operation. She was able to carry out these activities without detection because she used remote servers throughout the world, in doing so she was able to access the "Dark Web", an unregulated, encrypted, anonymous part of the internet. Some of the horrors she had found ensured she did not

make it a habit to make frequent visits to this ghastly entity.

"Well," Pegg continued, "here it is, see what you can tell me about it." Pegg gave her a slip of paper with the telephone number written on it.

"I'll have a bit of a play with it after. Now let's finish our lunch."

After they'd finished and Angie had put the things away. She went into her office, which was the house's original dining room. The room had several items of IT equipment installed in it; amongst the items were two desktops. a couple of laptops, and some printers and scanners. She sat down at one of the terminals and started tapping on the keyboard.

Pegg said, "Whilst you are doing that, I'll check on Catherine Rose."

"Do that Archie. Perhaps you can get her dressed to go out, there's a coat and some trousers in her wardrobe. I'll get this in motion, and it can work at it whilst we're out."   Pegg went upstairs and into the child's room. She was awake and as Pegg came in she pulled herself up and stood up with her hands holding the side of her cot. The little girl was now fourteen months old. She had almost white curly hair, and deep blue eyes. There was so much of Angie and Cath in her, Pegg thought. Although Pegg was unrelated to her by blood, as far as he was concerned, he was her Grandpa.

"Da! Da! Da!" she squealed, as Pegg approached the cot.

Pegg lifted her out of the cot and kissed her baby brow.   "We are all going to the park, you, me, Mummy and Fred. How would you like that?"

"Da! Da! Da!"

By this time, the poodle had joined them. Pegg let her down and she toddled over to Fred and put her arms around his neck. The animal reciprocated the greeting by gently licking one of her arms.

"Right young lady, do you need a change of nappy, before we stick some outdoor clothes on?" A quick check showed the child was a bit damp.

Pegg changed her and put the trousers and jacket on. They went downstairs, he put her down and she toddled off to the living room, followed by Fred. Angie left what she was doing, she let the programme run, and stood up, closed the office door, and joined them in the living room.   They walked from the house to the recreation ground just off Haspalls Road. Pegg pushing the child's buggy, whilst Angie had Fred on his leash. Once they arrived at the rec, they went over to the fenced off play area. Angie let Fred off his leash, and commenced throwing a ball which the excited, yapping animal retrieved, and running back to her, dropped it at her feet. The action was repeated several times. Pegg meanwhile had entered the play area and released Catherine Rose from the confines of her buggy. She toddled over to the swings where Pegg lifted her onto the seat, which was more like a small crate, with openings at its front to accommodate small legs. After securing the child in the seat, he stood in front of her and gently pushed her seat, causing the swing to go backwards and forwards. The resultant shouts and squeals were testament to her enjoyment. They moved on to some of the other rides. The little girl was unafraid of climbing up onto slides and seesaws. They spent a further hour on the rec before walking back to Angie's house.

Once in the house Angie went back to her office, whilst Pegg played with Catherine Rose in the sitting room. After a lapse of some twenty minutes Angie joined them again. She had a printout in her hand.

"Archie this is interesting, the number you gave me is nothing very unusual, considering the suspected nefarious nature of the user At least I suspect there must be something moody about it, otherwise you would not have given it to me to look at."

"What have you found out?" said Pegg as he got up from the floor.

"Well the phone is registered to a company that's based in Nottingham. I googled it and the address comes down to a wholesale clothing company, I've written down the address. The account is not in an individual's name, but in that of the company. I expect it is a contract account with the phone provider, and possibly one of several phones. I have also listed calls made to and from that phone. It's all written down"

"I really appreciate this Angie," said Pegg taking the paper and putting it in his pocket, "and as soon as I can I'll let you know what this is all about."

Pegg stayed on longer than he intended, but Angie was glad of his company. He had an evening meal with her, having previously put the little girl to bed and read her a story. She had fallen asleep before he'd finished it. It was eight o'clock by the time he left Angie's house. He arrived back at his house within thirty minutes. There were several messages on the answering machine.

CHAPTER 7

Pegg got a note pad and started to play back the messages, the first read:

"Archie it's Jenny from the front office at Dereham, sorry to bug you on your day off, there is an American gentleman, a Major Tom O'Brien, he'd like to speak to you, he said it was quite important here are his contact details…." He noted them down before erasing the message and moving onto the next one:

"Hello Archie, It's Mo, I'm sorry to have missed you. Just to let you know I have phoned the number the man called Ghazi gave me this morning. Perhaps we can talk about this, but not on the phone. Thank you so much for being there for me."

Pegg wrote down a few notes regarding this call, before erasing it and moving onto the next message:

"Hello sarge it's Mel Hobson. I'm really sorry to bother you, but I would like somebody to talk to regarding the fatal RTC we attended the other night. It's the thought of those little kids being orphaned and it's really getting to me. I know it sounds silly me going on about it. I think Matt is pretty cut up about it as well."

The other messages were just some cold calling, which Pegg erased. He picked up the handset from its cradle and dialled Mel Hobson's number:

"Hi Mel, it's Archie Pegg. How are things, I just picked up your message."

"Oh, sarge I'm sorry I feel such a wimp, I didn't mean to bother you."

"Stop it right there. First you are no bother, second, I'm pleased that you called. The RTC which we attended was a pretty traumatic incident even for an old sweat like me. We as police officers deal with some quite horrendous stuff, it is part of our job. The powers that be expect us to be detached and professional. The public expect it of us as well. But you must remember that under the uniform we wear, there is a human being, who has the same feelings and emotions as anyone else. But when we're together just ourselves that is, well we can let our guard down. I said you can call me any time if you want to. I will ensure that I am in the loop regarding the welfare of those kids. Anything I find out you will be the first to know. Now what are you doing tomorrow?"

"Well I'm still on my rest days, I was thinking of going out with mum, but I do not feel up to it."

"Why don't you and Matt come over and have some lunch, I'll fetch you and take you home again, that way you can have a couple of drinks. I'll call Matt if you want."

"No, I'll let him know he doesn't live too far from me."

"That's great I'll see you at yours at about midday.
Listen Mel it'll be okay. I've been there as well you know."

"Thank you I really appreciate your time."

They spoke for a further ten minutes. Pegg ended the call.   He dialled the number Tom O'Brien had given:

"O'Brien, who's speaking?"

"Sergeant Archie Pegg, I had a request from you through our front office that you wished to speak to me on a matter of some importance."

"Archie, I called your office, I wanted to speak to you personally, but I was told that you were on rest days, and that they would not give me your private telephone number without your permission. I really appreciate you taking the time to speak to me on your days off."

"No problem, sir, how can I help?"

"I have been able to get quite a bit done regarding the deaths of Mario and Lucia, and for the future welfare of the twins. I could not have expedited the situation as quickly as I did without your help. I carried out the formal identification of Mario and Lucia. We were able to assist the pathologist by making available the medical records of them both. This greatly assisted the pathologist in the sad process. The autopsies have been completed and the Coroner has given permission for Mario and Lucia's bodies to be released to the USAF North Wendlesham. In due course we will
arrange for them to be repatriated to the States.'

'A police officer called the Collision Investigator called our Base Headquarters and gave us a heads up on what had caused the crash. From the sound of it, Mario hit a patch of ice just as he was breaking to negotiate a righthand swing, and he lost it, went off the highway flipped the car and hit a tree.'

'Our own medical examiner was present at the autopsies, and the Norwich Hospital Pathologist was assisted by our guy. As a result of this, preliminary cause of the deaths was deemed to be massive trauma. Death was almost instantaneous in both cases. It is not believed that either of the deceased had consumed drugs or alcohol. We are waiting on toxicology reports to confirm this. The Coroner has opened and adjourned an Inquest. The Inquest will resume at a later date.'

'Finally, I'd like to tell you what is happening regarding the twins, Gino and Guilia. Thanks to you the children will not be taken in by Social Services. They were quite happy that we would take care of them, pending future arrangements."

"How are they?" asked Pegg.

"Well considering what they've been through, they are okay. They were treated for inhalation of gasoline fumes.

Fuel had leaked through their clothes and onto their skin, they had a few bruises, but being strapped into the car seats had saved them from further injury. But the thing that got me was that if you and your colleagues had not got those kids out of the car when you did, they could have been burnt to death."

"Well don't dwell on it, sir, we were there, and we pulled them out, and the car did not catch fire, "Pegg reassured him, "so where are they now?" he asked.

"Well my wife June is looking after them, at our house on the base. Both our kids are in the States, one at college the other at university, so we've got plenty of room. The twins know June, and they've visited us before, at various social dos we had. Mario and Lucia were regular visitors. Hell, I was mentoring Mario for applying to get a commission, he was soon to be promoted to Technical Sergeant. He was studying to get into the Air Force Academy in Colorado. I feel I owed it to him and his wife, and now it's all gone. I'm am so angry and sad at the same time, it's such a terrible waste."

They talked for a few more minutes before O'Brien ended the call. It was gone half past nine. Pegg decided to have an early night. There was a lot to do in the morning, and an early start was needed. He let Fred out into the garden whilst he went and had a quick shower.
After this he locked up and went to bed.

CHAPTER 8

Pegg was up early. After breakfast he took Fred for a walk around the village for twenty minutes, he then drove into Dereham, and did some food shopping, when he'd finished, he gave Mo a call on his mobile.

"Hi Mo, it's Archie Pegg, where are you at the moment."   "I've just got in to work, I'm alone in the office doing some paperwork. The shop is not yet open."

"I'm parked up in the Cowper Road car park, can we meet?"

"Great, come around to the back door, and I'll let you in."   Two minutes later they were sitting in Mo's office. Pegg told him what he had found out about the telephone number.

"It seems that the people behind this are not too fussy about security, there was no sign of any encryption. The number is down to a bog-standard phone whose provider is one of the national networks. In fact, the account which this phone is part of, is one of several phones owned by the company," explained Pegg.

"What company is this?"

"Well it's a wholesale clothing company, Fashion Trends, it's based in Nottingham."

"I have never come across them."

"I'm not surprised Mo. They cater for small stallholders, market traders and the like. Now tell me what happened when you called the number your unwanted visitor gave you."

"Well I called the number at about half past eight, it was answered by a guy, who when I said who I was, he spoke Farsi. He said that he would be in touch, and then he hung up."

"Will he call on your mobile, office or home phone?"
"Mobile, I assume, that is the only number he would have."

"No specific time-frame?

"No, just that he would be in touch."

"Right here's what I'm going to do, but only if you want me to, okay?"

"As long as my parents continue to be safe, you can do whatever you want."

"I've got some contacts in Nottingham, not police by the way, who I will get to make some discreet enquires about the guys who run Fashion Trends. In the meantime, Mo, try and not to worry too much, we'll get through this together.
And if I can, I will nail these bastards."

Pegg left Mo and returned to the Land Rover. He called an acquaintance in Nottingham. Afrim Babic was an ethnic Albanian but was born in Kosovo. His family had been slaughtered in the 1990's conflict between the Serb forces and Kosovar rebels. Babic was a young boy then he fled south and stayed in a refugee camp, run by the British Army. He was befriended by some of the soldiers who ran the camp.

He was eventually accepted as a refugee in the UK, and consequently was granted UK citizenship. He first encountered Pegg, as a result of being coerced into causing Pegg near fatal harm. Pegg managed to get Babic away from the clutches of the thugs that Babic was involved with and was able to get the young man's business back on track. This resulted in a deep bond between the two men.

"Hello Afrim, it's Archie Pegg, how are you my man?"
"Archie! So good to hear from you! I'm good, how are you, and how is my special friend Fred?"

"We're both fine."

The conversation continued, first it was a catch-up. Babic's business enterprises had expanded. As well as running three hand car washes, he had also opened a convenience store. In addition, he had plans for a DIY store. Babic had come a long way since his original car wash had been stolen from him by a rogue solicitor, with the help of this corrupt advocate's henchmen. The solicitor, having been struck off by the Law Society, was now serving a lengthy jail sentence, his henchmen had fled to their native country, Albania. Pegg had enabled the car wash to be returned to its rightful owner, Babic, and since then the enterprise had flourished. Finally, Pegg asked:

"Afrim, I need some help. I don't know if you are able to assist me."

"Of course, Archie, I will help in any way I can. What is it you want me to do for you?"

"I have a friend who is in some serious shit, from some very bad people. I can't tell you too much at this stage as people's lives could be in danger. But to start with I need an address checking out. If you feel that you can't do this, then I understand."

"Tell me where this place is. Is it far away from me?"
Pegg gave him the address and the name of the company, Fashion Trends.

"I know this area; it is a place where there are lots of small businesses which supply the retail trade. I get some of the stuff for my convenience store from this estate."
"Here's what I'd like you to do. I want you to check the place out, but be careful, I do not want people to get the idea that you are snooping around. It is important that they do not catch onto the real reason as to why you are there. I mean you could pretend that you are looking for a supplier for one of your businesses. I'll leave it to you. I want to know the name of the person who runs the enterprise. What it is they do exactly, where do they get

their stuff from. The type of guys who work there, that sort of thing. Do you think you can do that for me?"

"Sure, I can; when do you want me to do this?"   "Well obviously you've got to run your work stuff, but if you can get it done for me as soon as you can."

"Sure, I do that for you Archie. How shall I get the stuff I find out back to you?"

"Get it all down on an email. That way it does not matter what time of day you get back to me. You've got my email address, haven't you?"

"Yes."

"Right I'll leave it with you. Remember don't let these Fashion Trends folk get any hint that you are fishing for information about them, just play the hard-working entrepreneur that you are that should not be difficult! Take care now Afrim, we'll speak soon."

Pegg ended the call. He drove the Land Rover out of the car park. He called in at one of the towns supermarkets and bought some rolls and ingredients to make up a salad, as well as some bottles of beer and a couple of bottles of wine. When he had completed his shopping, he drove off to Mel Hobson's address. When he arrived, Matthew Boggis was already there. After a brief conversation, they got into

Pegg's Land Rover and travelled back to Pegg's house. It was a bit after midday by the time Pegg had parked up. After Pegg had settled the young officers in the lounge, he gave them some drinks, a beer for Boggis and a glass of wine for Hobson. He got himself a beer and joined them. He was anxious to let the Boggis and Hobson to start talking about the fatal single vehicle collision they all had attended a couple of days ago. He wanted them to initiate the conversation.

"Okay guys, here's to us," said Pegg raising his glass, before continuing, "I want you to consider this a safe place, and anything that is said here, does not get mentioned outside these walls by me, unless you give your consent.

The reason I've got you here is not only to have some lunch and a few drinks, but for you speak about what just happened on the last set of nights. I know that things can get on your mind, and after a bit they take over and eventually they get a hold of you to the detriment of your home and working lives. Believe you me, I've been there." The other two said nothing, they sipped their drinks. After a bit, Boggis said:

"I keep thinking about those little kids, and their dead parents. What's going to happen to them, all alone in the world. If we had been at the scene sooner, maybe we could have done something for their mum and dad."

"Look," said Pegg, "there was nothing to be done for them, they were dead before you two arrived on scene. But you did make a difference with the children. They are alive thanks to the efforts of you both. So, don't forget that."

"Do you know what's happening with the kids, now they are orphaned," asked Hobson.

"Well they are currently being looked after by Mario Posetti's Deputy Squadron Commander, Major O'Brien and his wife, at their house on the air base. The O'Briens knew the parents and the kids have been to the O'Briens' together with their parents, on several occasions. So, they are not going into any children's home or orphanage. I think that the authorities are contacting relatives in the States; no need to worry, they are in a loving home environment."

Pegg had ascertained that neither Boggis nor Hobson had been so close to a fatal traffic accident before. They had in their short careers come across dead people, but these were incidents were sudden deaths, which mainly involved elderly persons, there were of course suicides and industrial accidents. Pegg went on to explain that it was easier to talk to somebody about events of a traumatic nature, rather than to let them weigh you down, thinking them over to yourself.

Pegg sometimes regretted the demise of police station canteens. They were a place to go after a shift and wind down, and in some cases have a glass of something before going home, and if an officer had been involved in an incident of a particularly unpleasant nature, it could be shared and maybe with a bit of support and banter, things could be made lighter of. There were a lot of things wrong with the old canteen culture, but there was a lot that was good about it as well. The PC Brigade had certainly thrown the baby out with the bathwater.

"Right let's get some grub into you two," Pegg said getting up.

"Matt sort out some drinks, I'll not have anything more yet."

Whilst the other two got some more drink, Pegg prepared the meal, finally setting the food on the kitchen table. After laying out three places, he called out to the living room, and the other two came in and sat down.

As they ate Pegg explained half the problem with unpleasant incidents is that folk do not want to talk about them, especially if they've been involved. Sometimes a person cannot deal with it on their own, and if they hold back and don't share it, then it's going to weigh them down, and eventually it can lead to serious problems, such as anxiety and even worse, depression. Sometimes it may not be enough to speak with friends or colleagues, and some form of professional support will be needed. It is a start to speak to someone first at a much more local level. After they had finished eating, they helped Pegg clear away, and the young officers retired to the front room again. Pegg fed the dog, who after he had finished eating settled himself down on Hobson's lap.

Pegg had gone out to fetch some more beers from the garage. When he came back, he said:

48

"Chuck him off Mel if you're uncomfortable, he's reverting to type, typical Poodle lapdog. He's gross after he's had some grub, licking his chops and belching, and you
getting a face full of dog's breath."

"Oh, don't be like that, he's fine, aren't you boy," she said.   The dog looked at Pegg and glanced up at Hobson, and snuggled down, giving a big sigh as he did so.

"Little tart," muttered Pegg.

They spent the rest of the afternoon, talking and reflecting what had been discussed. It was getting on for five and time for them to leave. They gathered their things together and clambered aboard the Land Rover. Pegg drove back to
Swaffham where he stopped outside Hobson's house, Boggis got out as well, before they went on their way, Pegg said:

"I hope that you will take on board what I've said, as John
Donne the poet wrote, "No man is an Island," that quote is as relevant today as it was when he wrote it over 400 years ago."

They said their farewells and Pegg drove back to Gressenhall. When he had got back, he took Fred out for a walk, up and down East Bilney Road, before returning to the house. On his return in he saw that there was a message on the telephone answering machine.

CHAPTER 9

"Archie it's Angie, can you get back to me on skype, using that app I installed on your PC."

After Pegg had successfully, with Angie's assistance, helped his old comrade, Tony Spratt to clear his name after he was accused of war crimes in the Balkans. Angie had suggested that it would be an idea that any communications between them regarding like matters in the future, should be secure. Angie had modified an app, which she had installed on her customers IT systems. It was a handy tool for businesses to use when they were communicating about confidential matters. It was common knowledge that some aspects of IT were not secure. The app allowed conversations and other communications to be encrypted. Pegg switched on his PC and logged on. He selected the Skype app, and clicked onto the secure mode, after which he dialled Angie. Her face appeared on the screen; she was in her office.

"Hi Archie thanks for getting back to me. I've been doing a bit of research regarding that number you gave me. Do not ask me how I did it. So here it goes. First, I have managed to extract some voicemail messages, unfortunately there is very little English used. I'm not a linguist, but I do not think the language or languages are European. I have put the recordings on a memory stick."

"Gosh Angie you're a genius! What else have you got?"

"Well interestingly, one of the numbers I found on the caller's list had 15 digits, which tells me it's a satellite phone. The country code within this number is 98, which is Iran. There were another two numbers which had the country code of 961 which is Lebanon, and 963 which is Syria. So, it appears that the person using the phone with the number that you gave me, is making calls to Iran, Lebanon, and Syria as well as receiving calls from those countries. I mean it could be that they are calls to family members, but the use of a satellite phone is not something an individual would normally own, as calls to and from these devices are very expensive. Normally it would be public companies or government agencies, who would be the users.

"Any idea who the account holder of the satellite phone is?"

"Well, the three main providers are Iridium, Immarsat and Globalstar, I think the provider for this satellite phone looks like Inmarsat. Now I've got the number I can do some research and find out about the account holder."

"Where's Ross? Does he know about what you are doing?"

"Oh, he's back, but he's in the living room watching the football, I often work a bit late in my den. He assumes I'm doing stuff for my clients. He has strict instructions not to disturb me when I'm in here. I feel a bit of a cheat doing all this stuff behind his back, but I do not want him involved, as he will probably put his parts on if he finds out what I'm doing. No one will ever find out as I cover my electronic footprints. It's all illegal this hacking, but what the heck, I need a bit of excitement in my life, Archie!"

"I'm in the same boat, but as you know when we bend the rules, it's all in a good cause. I'll let you know as soon as I can what this is all about. You'll see why I've been so reticent about giving too much away."

"What are you doing tomorrow?"

"I'm back on days, so I'll be starting work at 7 am."

"I've got to come to Dereham tomorrow, I'm seeing a client on Greens Road Industrial Estate, I'll drop an envelope off at the Police Station."

"That'll be great, just leave it at the front office, I don't know if I will be in or not. If I am, I'll come and see you." Pegg disconnected the Skype app. He decided to phone Mo.

"Hello Archie, what can I do for you at this late hour."

"I'm sorry to phone this late, but I really need to meet up with you again. I am working days, but I'm wondering if you could come and see me at home, tomorrow evening, or some other day this week?"

"Tomorrow should be okay, what time are you thinking of?"

"About seven?"

"That'll be okay, what's it about"

"I don't want to say too much over the phone, but I've done quite a bit of research on that thing you gave me, and I need your input. Oh, and before you come, leave your mobile at home"

"Why Archie?"

"Well maybe I'm a bit paranoid, but your whereabouts can be traced through your phone. I do not want anyone to know you've been here. It may be the case that your phone is okay, but I'm not prepared to take any chances. Leave the phone at home if it's switched on any messages will go to voicemail."

"Okay that's fine, I'll see you then." Mo paused before he continued, "Archie, I've something to say to you. Esi knows about the threat to my parents." Pegg said nothing. "Archie are you still there?" After a further pause, Pegg said:

"Mo you've put me in a very difficult situation. Esi is a lawyer, I am not too happy with having him in the know. Where is he with this?"

"I do not think you have to worry; he is aware of the danger to Mama and Papa."

"In which case I would like him to come as well, as I need to explain a few things to him before we get going on this. Will he come as well?"

"Just a minute, I'll have a quick word." There was a pause of a couple of minutes before Mo came back,

"Archie he'll be with me."

"I'll see you both at seven tomorrow then. Oh, and by the way the mobile phone ban applies to Esi as well." Pegg gave Mo his address and postcode, after which he ended the call.

Pegg was concerned that the involvement of Mo's partner could unravel his plans. If Esi was going to have his lawyer's head on, it will not bode well regarding the outcome of this sad situation. He would have to lay it on

52

the line, if Esi is involved, there could be serious implications for the solicitor, regarding his future as a practising advocate. Pegg was clearly thinking of abandoning the whole thing. The stakes were becoming too high. He went through in his mind what had been achieved so far. The information which had been gleaned so far, revealed that there was a connection between Iran, Syria, Lebanon, and the UK. Hopefully more gaps will be filled in once Pegg knew what the information Angie had downloaded onto the memory stick.

Tomorrow he had an early shift, so he decided to turn in. He let Fred out whilst he made up a lunch box for work. After letting the dog in, he locked up, showered, and went to bed.

CHAPTER 10

Pegg was up, washed, and dressed by six o'clock. He had an arrangement with a neighbour, who would look after Fred for the day. He walked the dog around the Green before calling on the neighbour at half past six. After leaving Fred, Pegg returned to the house. He collected the bag which contained his food and other sundries and locked the house up, before driving to Dereham police station.   After parking up, he entered the building, and made his way to the sergeants' office where he was briefed by the night shift sergeant. The main incident overnight had been a series of thefts in the town, where diesel been taken from fuel tanks of mainly commercial vehicles. A couple of transport hauliers had their yards targeted, and fuel had been syphoned out of LGV tanks. In addition, several vehicles parked outside the units of an industrial estate had also had fuel taken from them. Pegg would get an officer to visit the premises and look at CCTV, and if necessary, get recordings of any useful footage. There were a couple of campaigns that the Division was running, seatbelts, and excessively noisy exhausts.

Pegg noted a couple of things down, and with the notes attached to a millboard, he went to the briefing room. All the Dereham early shift were there, he phoned Swaffham section, and put the call on speaker, all three Swaffham officers, including both Boggis and Hobson were present. For the next fifteen minutes Pegg gave a rundown on what had happened overnight, and the campaign on seatbelts and noisy exhausts. He detailed a couple of officers to visit premises which had been hit with diesel thefts, with the idea of obtaining useful CCTV images. He issued them both with some spare USB sticks and CDR discs. When he'd finished with the briefing he said to the assembled officers: "Right guys, let's get to it, and hey, watch your backs and be careful out there!"

The officers got up and went their various ways, Pegg meanwhile went upstairs to CID. There he spoke to the DS and appraised him of the upsurge in diesel thefts. The DS believed that the perpetrators could be a team working out of King's Lynn. Cambridgeshire police had said that there had been a lot of thefts in the Wisbech area, which was just over the county border. Customs roadside checks, where officers were dipping fuel tanks, had cut down the amount of thefts of dyed or untaxed diesel. That was a relief to the hard-pressed agricultural industry, but of no comfort to the current victims of fuel theft, hauliers and the like. Pegg noted down some intelligence regarding the possible thieves and returned to the sergeants' office.

He went to his pigeonhole, and carried its contents to his desk, and started to go through the sheets of paper, files, and crime reports. He assigned crime reports to officers and entered the details onto the IT system. He read through a couple of crime files, and signed them off, before putting them into the mail room's CPS pigeonhole. When he had returned to his desk, his phone rang: "Archie, it's Jenny in the front office, Angie Mason just called in, she's dropped off a jiffy bag for you."

"I'm on my way, is she still there?"

"No, she's gone; she sends her apologies, but she was running a bit late, and had to see someone in Dereham, business I think."

Pegg put the phone down and went to the Front Office. Jenny, the Public Enquiry Office clerk, gave him an A5 size Jiffy bag. After exchanging pleasantries, Pegg returned to his office again. He opened the bag and emptied its contents onto the top of his desk. There was a USB memory stick and a couple of sheets of paper, on which Angie had typed a brief description of the contents of the stick. She had concluded by writing:

"Archie, please do not use your police computer terminal to read the enclosed memory stick. IT at Force

Headquarters will definitely be able download is contents, if you want to keep all the moody stuff which I've hacked for you to between us, wait until you get home, and use your own PC. Keep safe. Angie."

Pegg read Angie's report once more, after which he put everything back in the Jiffy bag and put it in his holdall. He managed to clear his paperwork during the next hour, after which he decided to take a walk through the town centre. He put on his stab vest, jacket, and cap, and walked out of the station. He spent the next hour and a half in the town centre. It was quite busy in town.

He was walking through the High Street, when he heard a cacophony of thumping bass music from behind him. He looked round to see a small red SEAT car amongst the slow-moving line of traffic. There appeared to be four young men in the car. The cars windows were all open, and the driver had his right hand out of the window and tapping it to the beat of the music. It was at this time the young man decided to rev the car's engine. The resulting din clearly showed that the cars exhaust was excessively loud. Pegg stepped out into the road, he waved the traffic on until the SEAT was in front of him. Pegg pointed to the side of the road, and indicated for the young driver to pull in.   The driver appeared to be from the London area, judging by his accent, he had a cocky attitude, especially after hearing Pegg's Norfolk accent. After giving the young man advice, and the appropriate ticketing regarding the vehicle's exhaust, and the sound level of the car's music system, Pegg sent the car and its young occupants on their way. He pondered if the young Londoner would be playing "Jack the

Lad" again, having come off worse after his run in with a "carrot cruncher copper".

Pegg continued his foot patrol through the centre of the town, engaging members of the public, in small talk and some friendly banter, and dispensing advice in response to the questions he was asked. After a two-hour absence from the station, he was back in the sergeant's office.

He removed his jacket and stab vest and walked to the Constables' Report Room. The two officers, who he had previously tasked to collect CCTV regarding the fuel thefts, were sitting down viewing the images from the collected clips.

"Any useful stuff yet."

"Not yet skipper, we've only just started."

"I can't afford to have you guys doing this. You need to get the video clips you've obtained up to the DS. He's got the resources to go through that stuff. Just write down where you got the images from and label the stick or disc as appropriate. Well done both of you for collecting all that material. After you've done that go and work on some of those crime reports I've left in your pigeonholes." There was about only an hour left of the shift and Pegg left the officers to it.

CHAPTER 11

Afrim Babic had also been busy. After his conversation with Archie Pegg a couple of days previously, he had been doing some investigating of his own. He commenced by doing some research on-line. Fashion Trends it appeared, did not trade as a retail enterprise.

The website proclaimed that *"We at Fashion Trends supply the trade with budget clothing, that does not scrimp on quality."* The clothes which the company supplied ranged from jeans, T-shirts, and other tops, to footwear and children's' clothing. The clientele were market traders and small independent shops. There was not much about the actual infrastructure of the company. There were no illustrations to show the exterior or the interior of its premises.

He had a genuine reason to visit the company as he was toying with the idea of stocking some items of children's clothing in his convenience store.

He visited the Companies House website, it was from here he was able to extract details of ownership, and when the company was incorporated. The business was started up four years ago, and it had connections with the UAE, but was registered in the Isle of Man. The only director he could find was a person called Akbar Mashrani. There were no records of bankruptcies, and Mr Mashrani had not been disqualified from running a company. He made a note of these details and logged out.

The same day as Pegg had started his day shift, Babic had begun his day by visiting his three car washes, and getting feedback from his employees, before returning to his convenience store, where he had an office at the back of the shop. It was from here that he ran his businesses. He made a list of clothing that he wished to order from Fashion Trends. The age range of the items he was thinking of stocking varied from 8 to 10-year-olds, down to new-born. After he had completed the list, he printed it off, and put it in a small messenger bag.

He left the premises in a small car derived van and drove to the industrial estate where the Fashion Trends premises were located, and where the other wholesalers he currently used were. He drove into the business park. The park covered a large area, at its entrance there was a board which displayed the names of the businesses and their locations within the park. He found where the company he was seeking was and continued into the estate. Fashion Trends was situated on the left, towards the end of a side road within the central part of the business park. At the end of the road there was a chain link fence, which backed onto the railway. On either side of the access road there were other units. Fashion Trends occupied the space of three units. It was bigger than Babic first thought. There were a number of vehicles parked outside the front some cars, a couple of small vans similar to the one Babic was driving, there were also two DAF 7.5 tonne box vans, one of which was backed up to the roller shutter door in the centre of the premises. They were both white, one had the company details painted on the outside of cargo section, whilst the other was just plain white. He took out his phone and whilst feigning a phone call, surreptitiously took photographs of the vehicles and the front of the premises. He noted that the plain white van had a loading platform fitted to its back end.

He parked up next to the plain white DAF box van and got out, taking the messenger bag with him, he made his way to a door marked "Customer Entrance" and entered. Babic had come into an enclosed space which had a counter running its entire width, behind the counter there was a halfglazed door. Opposite the counter on the other side of the room there was another door. Through the half glazed door, he could see a couple of people sitting behind their workstations, one was a young woman, and the other was a man in his 30s or 40s. They appeared to be of South Asian, or maybe of Middle Eastern heritage. On the walls around the reception area there were posters showing models wearing what would appear to be examples of the type of clothing the company had on offer. Babic's attention was drawn to pictures of children's clothing, especially those showing toddlers and infants. There appeared to be some good quality merchandise on offer. Babic walked around the looking closely at the posters. As he was doing this, he heard door behind the counter opening. He turned around and the man he had previously seen through the half-glazed door.

"Good morning, I'm Michael, how can we help you, today?" the man said; he spoke in heavily accented English.

"Yes, good morning to you too," said Babic. "I would like to see some of your children's clothing, especially for toddlers and infants. I am thinking of selling this sort of merchandise in my shop."

"We believe we can supply what you are looking for, what sort of quantities are you looking to sell?

"Well I have made up a list of the type of stuff I'm looking for," said Babic taking the list he had printed off earlier out of the messenger bag.

Michael took the list and read through it, before returning it to Babic.

"Yes, I think that we can supply most of the items that you are looking for."

"I'd like to see and feel the quality of the clothing before I make a decision as to whether I should place an order with you."

"Of course, but before I take you through to the back, what is the address of your shop."

Babic was not surprised at this request, there are a lot of timewasters about. And of course, there was the low life who would be casing properties with a view to breaking in and making off with some very easily saleable merchandise. Receivers always had a ready market for under the counter clothing. He gave Michael the name and address of his shop. Michael went through the door to the office again. Babic saw him at his workstation and tapping on his keyboard. He was checking the on-line classified directory, I bet, thought Babic. A couple of minutes later, he returned. "Come with me Mr Babic."

Michael led Babic through the door opposite the counter, and into a warehouse area, it was quite a sizable space area. He had seen from the outside that the premises occupied three unit's worth of space. The interior of the building he could see that two of the sections consisted of shelving upon to which were stacked cardboard boxes. There were also wheeled racks on which were hung dresses, tops, T-shirts, and trousers. The final section was partitioned off, not by a brick wall, but by a wooden frame onto which was fastened plywood sheets. In the middle of this partition there was a door, which was wide enough and high enough to enable stacked pallets to pass through it. From behind the partition came the sounds of banging and the whine of electric power tools.

Babic found this odd as it appeared that there was some sort of engineering workshop, which seemed completely out of place here in a clothing warehouse. The only vehicular access to the interior of the premises was an entrance with a closed metal roller door. This was in what was the middle of the centre section of the three adjoining buildings.

"Here we are," said Michael indicating to some shelving near to the back of the storeroom.

He took down half a dozen boxes from a shelf and laid them down on the floor.

"These contain examples of the type of clothing you may be looking for," the man continued.

He lifted the loose lids of the boxes to show their contents. Babić took out some items from one of the boxes they were baby grows. He took one out of its packaging and ran his fingers through the material.

"This is good stuff, and how much would a gross of this cost?"

"We can come to some arrangement with you, we try to keep our costs to our customers down."

"I would obviously pay the going rate, but my customer base is working people, and my shop is located on a public housing estate. Most of my customers are women who quite frankly struggle to keep their heads above water.
There are a lot of young mums who could do with a nearby kids clothing outlet."

"I think that you will be pleasantly surprised at our terms." Michael went on to show Babic further examples of their stock. The man's phone sounded, he answered it, speaking a foreign language.

"Will you excuse me for a minute, I'm needed in the office. Keep looking at our stuff, there are other items on the shelves next to where the ones I took down, I'll be back in a minute."

Babic continued looking through the boxes. He was looking through the toddlers' wear when he heard a shout from behind him. Babic looked up to see a tall slim man aged in his forties approaching him from the direction of the partition. He was of eastern Mediterranean appearance and had a neatly trimmed full beard. *"Aya mitavanem be shoma konam?"*

"I'm sorry, what did you say."

The bearded newcomer said, "I'm sorry, can I help you?" Babic stood up and held his hand out and said: "Afrim Babic, Michael was showing me some examples of your stock, but he was called away to the office. He told me to keep looking whist he was away; I am looking to place an order for some children's clothing."

"Sorry my friend, I did not realise this", the man continued in heavily accented English, "we have had problems with people stealing from us. I'm Akbar Mashrani, I am manager here. Mr Babic, that is not an English name you have."   "No, I am originally from Kosovo, but I've lived here since the age of 10. It's a long story, but I am now a UK citizen. I have my own businesses here. I have a lot to thank my adopted country for. If you don't mind me asking, I am not familiar with the language you first used, it was not Arabic." "No, I was speaking Farsi, forgive me I thought you were one of....", he paused, as if he were about to say something he shouldn't, he continued, "never mind enough of that. I do not want you here by yourself, so if you don't mind, please come with me back to the office." Before anything further happened, they were joined by Michael, who had obviously finished with whatever he had been called away for. Mashrani started to speak animatedly to Michael in another foreign tongue, but this time Babic knew what it was; it was Arabic. After he had finished berating Michael, Mashrani stormed off in the direction of the partition, opening the door, entering the space behind it and closing the door behind him.

Babic said, "I think I have seen enough of stuff you have on offer. I do not want you to get wrong with your boss again. Can you let me have some prices, and I'll email you an order? I am well pleased with the quality of clothing." "I should have realised Mr Mashrani would have been angry to find you in here by yourself. I apologize for that. He hasn't always been like that. It's only been for the past few weeks he has been very much on edge."

"I noticed he speaks Arabic to you."

"Yes, I am from Lebanon, Leila my colleague is Syrian, Mr Mashrani comes originally from Iran, but he speaks good Arabic."

"Well I'm Kosovan by heritage, it seems a bit like the

United Nations here!"

They went back to the reception area where Afrim was given a selection of children's clothing. He would place a larger order if he managed to sell the small selection he had just purchased. After driving back to his office. He set about writing an e-mail to Pegg. After sending all his findings, regarding Fashion Trends and their premises, he went back into the main part of the shop; with the help of one of the ladies, they set about unpacking the examples of children's clothing and putting the items on display.

CHAPTER 12

Pegg had finished his shift and was now back home, having picked Fred up from the neighbour. He made himself something to eat. After he'd finished his meal, and after clearing up, he got out his laptop. He opened his emails. There were several in the inbox. The only one which caught his attention was the one Babic had sent him, the rest he deleted. In his email, Babic had couched it in language expressing one retailer's view to another; any third person reading it would be led to believe it was a couple of shopkeeper's waxing lyrical about a new supplier. Pegg read what Afrim Babic had written:

My dear Friend,

As you know I explained about me expanding the lines in my shop, with a view to selling baby and toddlers clothing. I have some information that may help you in your endeavours in finding likewise merchandise. I visited a wholesaler called Fashion Trends; I can send you their contact details if you are interested. I attach a couple of photos I took of the outside of their premises, as you can see, they have a couple of vans, so they can deliver.

I have bought some examples of clothing which I have displayed in the shop. Staff at Fashion Trends were very kind and helpful, there are two in the office, Leila who is Syrian and a young guy from Lebanon called Michael. Michael had taken me into the warehouse to look at some of the kids clothing; as we were looking through some stuff, he had a call to go back to the office. There I was alone looking through some boxes of stuff when I heard a shout in a foreign language. A guy who seemed very wound up, asked me what I was doing. It turned out he was the boss, an Iranian called Akbar Mashrani. Anyway, when the poor Michael came back, Mr Mashrani was furious yelling at him in Arabic. After which he stormed off to another part of the warehouse which was partitioned off from the main part of the warehouse.

The funny thing was that from behind the partition there was a lot of noise from electric machinery and tools, as well as blue arc flashes, so somebody maybe welding. It sounded more like an engineering workshop than a clothing warehouse.

If my initial purchase goes well, and I have no reason to doubt it won't, then I'll go back to Fashion Trends and get a lot more.

If you need more information give me a call. Best wishes Afrim.

Pegg opened the attachments. The first one was a photograph of the whole frontage of the premises. There were four cars, a blue VW Polo, a red and a green Ford Transit Connect van, and finally a black BMW X5 SUV, whose front and rear side windows were tinted, as well as its back window. Pegg made a note of the vehicles' registration numbers. He then opened the second attachment. This was a photograph of two DAF 7.5 tonne box vans parked side by side, the plain white one was parked directly with its rear end in front of the roller shutters. He could see that this vehicle had a loading platform, whilst the vehicle parked beside it, the one with the company logo, did not. He noted the vans' registration numbers.   He got out an A4 writing pad and started to write down all the information he had so far. After which he got the jiffy bag which Angie had left for him. He slotted the USB stick into his laptop, he re-read the accompanying report.

Angie had written:

The first part of the recording is a message from the satellite phone with the Iran code 98, using the provider Immarsat. It was left on the voicemail of one of the mobiles belonging to the clothing firm. The next is the same phone calling the 963 code which is Syria. This is actually in English, very heavily accented but you can understand it. Then we have some calls made from the clothing firm's mobile to a 961 code which is Lebanon. They are all in a foreign language, which sounds different to first call from the Iran satellite phone.

The rest of the report was a list of calls made between Iran to the clothing firm, and Iran to Lebanon and Iran to Syria, and the clothing firm to Lebanon, and Iran. Pegg added these details to his notes on the A4 pad. He looked at his watch, it was an hour before his visitors were due. He put on a jacket and a cap, and took Fred for a walk around the Green, after which he fed him. He then set up the kitchen table for the meeting. He had his laptop ready for immediate access.

He heard a car pulling into the driveway, the gates of which he had left open. He went to the back door, which opens out from the kitchen. The sensor light on the outside wall illuminated the area between the garage and the kitchen door. Fred came behind him and started to bark. Pegg picked him up and held him in his arms. Mo got out of the driver's side, Esi Nzema was already out of the vehicle. He was a large proportionately built man, who Pegg always felt would not be out of place in a heavyweight boxing bout. Both men came to the door and greeted Pegg. The wriggling poodle was anxious to get down and greet the guests.

"Do you have any issues with dogs? If so, I'll put him in another room."

"No problems with us, "said Mo.

Pegg put the dog on the floor, and after greeting the two visitors, and having established that they were not a threat to him or Pegg, the poodle settled down in his basket.

"Well this is a first for me Mr Nzema, on previous occasions that we've met, I've either been in a custody suite, or I've been standing in the witness box, being cross examined by you. I am looking forward to speaking with you in a non-adversarial environment!"

"Two things Mr Pegg, it's Esi, and we are on the same side; not that we weren't on the same side as before, that is the side of justice."

"Touché, point taken, Esi, and I'm Archie by the way."
Pegg invited the two men to sit down at the table, before he continued:

"If we are going to help Mo, without putting the lives of his parents in danger. We are going to have to work below the radar so to speak. In doing so we will probably be breaking the law. I am sorry to have to put it like this, but we must have complete trust in each other. Esi, you and I are part of the criminal justice system. How are you about bending the rules and in some cases breaking the law in order to help Mo, and keep his parents safe and alive?"
"After Mo spoke to me about the way his parents could be persecuted by the authorities back in Iran, I have given

this a lot of thought, and I feel that this is one of those rare occasions where bending the rules for the greater good is entirely justified; to that end, I'm with you and Mo." "Good, I am not asking you to condone anything serious like murder or whole scale criminal activity. If we are to bring this episode to a satisfactory conclusion, we may have to at some time, involve the powers that be; but we will come to a decision on that only after Mo is completely happy that his parents are no longer at risk. Right, Mo has anybody called you since you agreed to go along with the people who you called?"

"Not yet, Archie."

"Okay let me tell you what I've dug up so far. The phone number which you were given to call by the man Ghazi is the number allocated to one of several mobile phones. The accountholder is a clothing firm which supplies retailers. It is located up in Nottingham. I'll tell you a little bit more about it in a minute. Now about this mobile phone number. I was able to find out a bit about the calls which were made from it. Amongst them was to a satellite phone located somewhere in Iran, and also calls to Lebanon and Syria."   "Gosh Archie, how did you get this stuff," asked Mo.

"At the moment I can't tell you," said Pegg before continuing. "I've managed to get hold of some recordings of voicemail messages left on the mobile number. I'm afraid most of them are in a language I do not understand. I'll play them back perhaps you could help me Mo."

"I'll try, let's hear them."

"Okay the first recording is from an Iran based satellite phone which leaves a message on one of the mobiles registered to Fashion Trends in Nottingham."

Pegg put the USB stick that Angie had given him into the laptop, and after it loaded up, Pegg played it back. Mo heard the first recording, after a couple seconds into the recording. Mo gasped and moaned:

"Na bad. Man mariz hastam."

Pegg stopped the recording, "What on earth is up, Mo." Mo said nothing. After a bit he said slowly:

"My God, Archie. The language is Farsi, my mother tongue. Not only do I know the caller's language, but I can tell you the bastard's name. It is the voice of Mehran Pejman. He is the person who stole my business in Iran and was involved in arranging the murder my partner.

Esi put his hand on Mo's arm, and whispered:

"We're all with you Mo, I know this is traumatic for you, but we need you to help Archie with what's on this recording."

"I'm sorry, I'll pull myself together," Mo said before continuing, "he says that he is sorry he missed you my brother, I need to speak urgently about the merchandise I arranged for our friend in Syria to send you. Call me as soon as you get this."

"Okay what is this Pejman guy, is he some sort of criminal gangster?" asked Pegg.

"Oh yes he is a criminal all right, but he is more than that, he is the local Guardian Commander in the area where I lived in Iran."

Pegg made some notes before continuing to play the next of the hacked voicemail recordings. Before he did so he said:

"Right we should all be able to understand the next voicemail, it's from the same satellite phone, but this time to a number in Syria, here goes." Pegg played the English language message:

"Hello, my friend, we are grateful for you supplying us with the material. But the machinery is complicated for us to use, get back to me as soon as you can."

"Well that was fairly straight forward, it did not sound as if it was the voice of Pejman did it?"

"That's right, it's not Pejman, it's probably one of his minions, I would say the caller was still Iranian." Pegg made some more notes, before saying:

"Right here's the next one. This came from the same mobile number Pejman, first called but this time it is to a phone in Lebanon."

Pegg played the recording. Mo asked him to play it a further three times.

"The language is not Farsi, it's Arabic. I am not a fluent Arabic speaker, but being born into a Muslim family, I do know a fair bit of the language. If you don't mind, if I could take a copy of the recordings, and I will write out a full English transcript for you. But the gist of the message is the caller asks the receiver can he have a progress report as to how the students are doing."

Pegg played the rest of the voicemail messages. They were all to the same Lebanese number. The last call was about the travel arrangements for the visitors. He made a note of the rest of the messages. Next, he took a spare USB stick, and sent the contents of Angie's stick to it. He gave the stick to Mo. He read through his notes, and then said:

"What we have got so far, is that the threats to Mo's parents are being made by Pejman, who is a commander in the Guardians or IRGC as we call it here, he is a murderer, and from the looks of it a very corrupt man. He is in contact with a clothing supplier in Nottingham. Now the manager of this company is a man called Akbar Mashrani, I believe he is of Iranian heritage. His firm's premises are located on a Nottingham industrial estate.

'My contact has visited these premises and they actually do supply clothing to the retail trade. There was one part of the warehouse which my contact could not get to see as it was partitioned off; but the curious thing about it was judging by what my contact says, it sounded like an engineering workshop. The only other people in the place that my contact could see were Arabs, namely a young Lebanese man and a Syrian girl. There were obviously people working in the partitioned off section, but we don't know how many."

"So, what do we do now?" asked Esi.

"Well if you could get a transcript of all those voicemail recordings done for me, Mo."

"Of course, I've got dictionaries at home, so I should get that done for you."

"Let me know when you've done it and I'll collect them from your office. Don't e-mail or post them to me. The other thing I'd like you to do is to go on some of the official Iranian government web sites and find out about the IRGC, and through that put in the names of Pejman and Mashrani, you never know you might get something. Also have a look through Iranian dissident cum resistance sites and we'll see what we can pick up about the IRGC types. I'm sorry if I sound paranoid, I've already got you leaving your phones at home, but when you do your searches of the Iranian websites, don't do them on a computer or tablet which can be traced back to you. For example, you could use an internet café or public library. I need to make sure that none of these bastards have an inkling of who you are or where you are from. The safety of Mo's mum and dad is paramount. Now unless you get a call about your warehouse from Nottingham. I suggest we re-convene here or at yours same time next week, I'll be on rest days."

"We'll meet at our place in Norwich," said Mo.

"That's fine, but if you get a call about the warehouse of yours in the meantime, we'll have to re-arrange things." After this they packed up, and Pegg's visitors departed. When they had gone Pegg got out a file cover, he proceeded to type up his notes. He wrote up a casual report on what information he had gleaned so far. He included locations, personalities, vehicles, and their numbers. After he had finished, he printed off a copy of what he written, and put it into the file. He put away his laptop and printer.

It was time to take Fred out for a final walk before he retired for the night. When he got back in, the house phone rang, it was Pat Warrington:

"Pat, to what do I owe this honour?"

"Archie, sorry to call at this late hour, but how are you fixed for the weekend? I'd like to come and see you again."   "You can come down any time. I am off from Thursday onwards."

"That's sounds great. I'm at a bit of a loose end, my department has a new project in the offing, it's something that I can't tell you about. The client is not yet ready for us to get going. So rather than twiddle my thumbs, I've booked some time off, I got a lot of leave owing."

"Why not come down tomorrow, I should be home by four. If I'm not you have a key, let yourself in. Are you bringing Zena, Fred will be pleased to see her?" Zena was Pat's German Shepherd bitch

"Not this time Archie, she's staying with mum and dad, it's a long story, but in brief, things have been a bit nasty in the village. There have been a lot of shady types about; these ne'er-do-wells have been cold calling on elderly folk, and touting for tree cutting, roof repairs and so on. And there have been a couple of break-ins to garden sheds. I think they are out from Sheffield, maybe Leeds or Bradford. We decided that Zena should remain with them. In any case she seems to be closer to mum than me." "Oh Pat, are they okay.?

"They are fine, Zena is fiercely protective of them. What better deterrent against unwanted visitors than a barking and snarling Shepherd!"

"I'll agree with that, we've got a few of those dogs on the
Force, they do a brilliant job."

72

"Well that's agreed then, I'll see you tomorrow then. She ended the call. Pegg got ready for bed. He slept well that night.

CHAPTER 13

The following morning, after Pegg had briefed the shift, he checked the numbers of the vehicles that Afrim had photographed at Fashion Trends. Two of them, the BMW X5 and the marked DAF 7.5 tonne box van, were registered to Fashion Trends, the others were leased from the same national leasing company. Pegg noted the details.

There had been some success with the ongoing fuel thefts investigation. CID had been going through the CCTV images and a couple of the thieves had been identified. The information had been passed onto the Fens Crime Investigation Team, which resulted in several addresses in West Norfolk and North Cambridgeshire being visited. Suspects had been arrested and bailed. Pegg knew that this would not be the end of it. Commercial vehicles would continue to be targeted; theft of diesel was an easy way for criminals to make money. Businesses really needed to up their game as regards to security. It was not as if they did not have enough problems keeping their heads above water, without having the hassle of bottom feeders stealing their vehicles' fuel.

He e-mailed the relevant crime prevention officers to remind their charges regarding fuel and vehicle security.

Pegg's mobile pinged; he had a text from Mo:

I've left an envelope for you. If you come to the sales counter one of the assistants will hand it over. Sorry that I will miss you, I am in Newmarket this morning. Back late pm if you want to speak. Mo.

Pegg decided to take a walk around the town centre. He informed Jenny in the front office before walking out of the station. He called in at Elite Clothing, and picked up Mo's envelope, after which he spent the next hour engaging with shopkeepers and members of the public. He moved on some recalcitrant drivers, who'd taken it upon themselves to park on double yellow lines. He returned to the station; Jenny had several people in the lobby of the front entrance waiting to be seen. Pegg gave her a hand to clear the queue, fifteen minutes later he was back in the Sergeants Office.

He opened Mo's A5 envelope. Inside were three typed sheets of A4 paper. Mo had written:

Archie, after a late-night visit to an internet café, I have gleaned some information which I hope will be useful. There are an awful lot of websites pertaining to the Islamic Republic, and Iranian dissident groups Contrary to popular belief, the internal politics are far from being homogenous. Like many autocracies, it seems that there are factions within the system, that seem to work against each other. I would not like to compare like with like, but in Nazi Germany, and in the Soviet Union, both Hitler and Stalin were more than happy to let their lieutenants compete among themselves, it ensured that their grip on power was absolute.

Sepeh-e-Pasdaran, or the Army of Guardians, known in international circles as the Iran Revolutionary Guards Corps (IRGC) is more than a security force. It has its tentacles in all aspects of Iranian life, as well as having its own armed services, which are separate from the Republic's Army, Navy and Air Force. There is also a specialist arm of the IRGC, which is known the Quds

Force. This is a part of the IRGC which engages in special and extra-territorial operations. They train and support organizations such as Hezbollah in Lebanon, and militias in Iraq, Syria, and Afghanistan. The commander of Quds Force is a very shadowy figure with the rank of a Major General.

I have also found out that the couple of names we had are in reality Quds Force officers. The manager of Fashion Trends Mashrani is a Colonel in Quds Force, whilst Ghazi is a major. Ghazi is officially an Agricultural Attaché at Iran's London Embassy. Please don't ask where this information comes from, but I assure you it's genuine. My gut feeling is that these guys, along with Pejman are working under the radar, and not with the official blessing of the Iranian authorities.

The other two sheets were translations of the voicemail messages which had been uploaded by Angie onto the USB stick. Mo had written:

Archie to continue, here are the transcripts of the voicemail messages from the satellite phone to the number in Lebanon.

This is the first one:

"Greetings my brothers. We are anxious to get the project finished. We need to know how our students are doing, and when their studies will be completed. Get back to me as soon as you get this." This is the next one:

"Greetings my brothers. Thank you for sending the progress report. When will the course be completed? We need an answer immediately." The final one reads:

"Greetings my brothers. Thank you for the information. Let me know your plan for the students' itinerary. It is essential they travel separately, and that they arrive at different airports/ports, and different dates and times. Tell me when all is arranged and finalized."

I hope that this will help. If I don't hear from you, I'll see you at our place in Norwich at the time and date previously arranged. Regards Mo.

Pegg read the notes again, before replacing them back in the envelope, which he put in his messenger bag. He made himself a cup of tea, after which he went to the post room and emptied the sergeants pigeon-hole. He returned to the Sergeants Office and proceeded to put the mail in the relevant sergeant's pigeonhole. The rest he put on his desk. He sat down, and sipping his tea, went through the paperwork. His mobile rang:

"Hi, I'm at yours, Archie."

"Pat, that's great, make yourself at home, I should be home in about two hours. Can you pick up Fred? He's at a neighbour's house. I'll phone him and let him know you're coming around." Pegg gave her the address.

"I'll do that, be a bit of company until you get back."

"I've got some food in the freezer, perhaps you could get something out to defrost." "I'm on it, catch you soon!"

Pegg ended the call and phoned the neighbour to let him know Pat will be picking up the poodle. After that, he finished what he was doing. When he had allocated some crimes to his constables, he returned to his desk. He was starting to realise the enormity of the task he had set himself in helping Mo resolve his problems with his mother and father. Unlike the problem Tony Spratt had, this difficulty had an international element to it. How on earth was he going to resolve it without involving official intervention? Any police or other agencies involvement would be putting the elderly couple's wellbeing at risk. He went through the information which he had gathered so far. Mo had been visited by an officer in the IRGC Quds Force, who was an accredited diplomat to the Iranian Embassy in London.

There was also another Quds Force officer who must be using the cover as a manager of Fashion Trends in

Nottingham. Mo's warehouse in Dereham is needed to store some items. What they are is not known at this stage. The man behind all of Mo's woes is Mehran Pejman, there is a link between Pejman, and the two Quds officers, Mashrani and Ghazi.

They are all members of the IRGC. From what Mo writes in his letter to Pegg, there are a lot of competing factions within the Iranian ruling hierarchy. Could they be part of a conspiracy to engineer some sort of incident which would put them in a good light with the upper echelons of the regime? Pure speculation at this stage, he thought. The voicemails showed that some sort of schooling or training has been going on with people in the Lebanon. The connection between Quds Force and the Lebanon is Hezbollah and its militias.

And then there was the voicemail left at the Syrian phone number, about the machinery being complicated to use. The link between this voicemail and the others, could be that the schooling or training is to do with the "complicated machinery." He would need to have eyes on the items which are going to be stored in Mo's warehouse. His thoughts were interrupted by the arrival of the late turn sergeant.

"Hello Archie, what do you say?" asked Janie Bellman.

"Oh, Janie, not a lot I'm afraid. There's precious little to hand over. There's been a bit of a result with the fuel thefts. The Fens Investigation team have carried out some raids, and they've nicked a couple of the thieves."

"Well that's good news, but I don't expect that'll be an end to it."

Pegg went on to tell her what else had happened during the day. After he'd finished, she said:

"Well that's nice to start the shift with a clean sheet so to speak."

Pegg waited for his shift to come back in, he phoned Swaffham to ask if they had any untoward incidents, but more importantly he wanted to check on Matt Boggis and Mel Hobson. Matt picked up the phone. Yes, it had been a busy shift, nothing too serious, a couple of minor traffic shunts, some livestock loose on the road and a few other things. Matt was fine, and Mel was okay. Pegg finished the call, and after packing his stuff away, he drove home.

* * *

The evenings were drawing out, so it was still quite light when Pegg drove into his driveway and parked the Land Rover next to Pat's X-Trail. After closing the driveway gates, the back door opened, and Fred rushed out to greet him. Pegg squatted and patted the dog's head and tousled his ears. He got to his feet again and made his way to the door where Pat was waiting. She had her dark hair in a ponytail, and she was wearing a pair of red cords and a blue sweatshirt. She was gorgeous, thought Pegg, what have I done to merit this beautiful woman's attention. When he got to her, he could see her brown eyes were moist, as if she were on the verge of crying. She wrapped her arms around his neck, and gave him a long and lingering kiss:

"Oh Archie, darling, I missed you so much," she murmured, relaxing her grip slightly

"I missed you too, sweetheart, come on let's go inside before the neighbours start talking."

He closed the door behind him. The kitchen was warm, and the accompanying aroma of cooking added to the cosy atmosphere.

"What time did you leave this morning, hon?" he asked.

"To tell the truth, I was already and packed before I called you, yesterday evening.

"That was a bit presumptuous of you Pat! Supposing I was tied up or something?"

She put her arms around his waist, and nestled her cheek against his chest and whispered:

"I knew that you would time for a lonely girl like me." Pegg hugged her and said:

"I've always got time for you. Mmm something smells good what have you got for us?"

"I've found some lamb cutlets in the freezer, so I've made us a hotpot. I've prepped some carrots and peas, that be okay for you?"

"Sounds great, fancy some wine with that? A nice bottle of Merlot?"

"Perfect, dinner should be ready in an hour."

"Right I'll pop upstairs and grab a quick shower and get changed."

"You do that, and I'll sort things out here."

Pegg went up to his bedroom. He noticed that Pat had unpacked and had left some of her stuff in the spare bedroom, but her dressing gown was on the back of his bedroom door. Pegg got out of his uniform shirt and trousers, hanging the trousers up in the wardrobe, and putting the rest of the clothes he'd been wearing in the laundry basket. He went to the en-suite bathroom and showered. He finished, dried himself and put his bathrobe on. He went into the bedroom only to find Pat there, wearing nothing but a smile. She walked over to him and put her arms around him and kissed him.

"Oh dear!" she said, "someone is pleased to see me! I think he needs some attention." She reached through his bathrobe and gently took hold of his hardness.

"Oh Pat!" Pegg gasped, "what about our dinner?"

"Dinner is temporarily delayed; I need a good seeing to Mr Pegg!"

She led him by his fully hardened maleness to the bed and threw back the covers, He took pf his bathrobe and joined her in the bed. They made passionate love, after which they lay in each other's arms. They made love once more before going downstairs, Pegg in his bathrobe and Pat in her dressing gown.

She had already laid the table, and she'd put the oven on again, to heat up the already cooked hotpot. The saucepans with the vegetables were now bubbling away.. Pegg rushed to the garage and brought in the bottle of wine.

"Brrr, it's perishing."

"I'm not surprised, you silly boy, you've hardly got a stitch on!

"Come here and warm me up then.

"We can fool about after, let's get our food sorted first." Pegg poured them a glass of wine.

"Here's to more fun Archie!"

"You are a naughty girl."

"Well sir, you'll have to sort this wayward miss out then, won't you? But now let's eat."

They ate their meal, and after clearing up, they retired to the living room with their glasses and the rest of the bottle of wine. Pat sat on the sofa, and Pegg sat on the armchair next to it. Fred decided this was the cue to leap onto her lap. Pegg started to remonstrate with the animal, but Pat told Pegg to relax. She tousled the poodle's topknot and started to fondle his ears. The dog looked at Pegg as if to say, "You're not the only one to have stolen this lady's heart." He sighed and with that sank his head down onto Pat's thigh, a look of utter contentment on his face.

"Now we sorted out our immediate needs, my dear lady, tell me all about the stuff that's been happening with you since we were last together," said Pegg.

Pat was a member of the research team at Sheffield University's faculty of Mechanical and Electrical Engineering. She talked about the stuff she had been doing before starting on the current project. They had done quite a bit of work already, but now things were on hold. The client was waiting for further finance to be sorted out. It was really good that she had got her teeth into something new and challenging.

She then went on to explain in more detail about the problems her parents and neighbours were having in High Bradfield her home village, west of Sheffield. They had been plagued by itinerants cold calling, and touting for tree lopping, roof repairs, and driveway paving, the callers got quite intimidating when people refused their services. Things had also started to go missing from gardens, ornaments, and planters, that sort of thing. There had been a couple of garden sheds being broken into, and garden machinery and tools being stolen. She decided to do something to help mum and dad deter these unwelcome visitors. She obtained a poster depicting a German Shepherd's head and shoulders, with the message under the photo, *"I LIVE HERE!"* Zena has quite a loud bark, and if there was knocking at the door her barking is quite deep and frenetic. That seemed to have done the trick, and things seem to have quietened down quite a bit.

The local police do their best, but with the city of Sheffield nearby and all that's going on there, they are a bit overwhelmed.

Another factor that seems to be reducing the visits of ne'er do wells are the activities of a real busybody and nosy parker, he is an elderly chap, who at one time used to be an officer in the Met. He's taken it upon himself, to more or less patrolling around the village, and asking strangers their business, and noting car and van numbers. Some of the traveller types tried to intimidate him, but he's a tough old bird and he was having none of it.

He gives a constant flow of information to the South Yorkshire Police's 101 number. Pegg was glad that things have started to get better for her parents. He mentioned that people with criminal intent loathe nosiness. Curtain twitchers and busybodies are more of a help than a hinderance to law enforcement agencies.

"Right tomorrow I have to work an early, and then I'll have a few days off. What are you going to do with yourself tomorrow?"

"I thought that I would look up Angie, I don't know what she'll be doing."

"Give her a call, the baby will be in bed, and she's probably chilling at this moment." Pegg dialled up her number:

"Hi Angie, I've got a visitor, who'd like a word, I'll hand you over to her." Pegg handed the phone to Pat.

"Hello Angie, it's Pat, how are things?"

Pegg could hear Angie's squeal through the phone's earpiece from where he was sitting. He left the women talking whilst he ushered a reluctant poodle off Pat's lap and into the kitchen.

"Come on boy, it's time to ease springs," he said opening the kitchen door. The dog trotted out and into the darkness setting off the sensor light as he passed the back of the garage. It was a clear and cold night. Frost overnight maybe, he thought. So, there will be a possibility of some minor shunts on the roads in the morning, especially those rural roads which never seem to get gritted. Oh well I shan't be bored. Fred came back from his foray in the garden. Pegg shut the door, he wiped the poodle's feet, and went back into the living room. Pat was still on the phone to Angie. She talked for a further ten minutes, before she ended the call.

"Well that's tomorrow sorted out," she said. "Angie's invited me over for the day."

"Oh, I expect that you'll have a lot of catching up to do." They stayed talking for the best part of an hour. Pegg was very conscious of the fact that he was keeping Pat in the dark about Mo's problems. After this they retired for the night. They went to bed, and after making love again, they both fell into a deep and undisturbed sleep.

CHAPTER 14

Afrim Babic was pleasantly surprised to find that the children's clothing he had begun to stock sold out very quickly. He decided to re-order. First, he held a consultation with the shop assistants. They told him which items sold well, and which other items they should add to the restocking order. Babic had re-organised the shop a bit to accommodate the clothing section, he had emptied one of the stock rooms. This would do for the time being. He really did not want to be looking for larger premises at this time. He picked up the phone and called Fashion Trends. The call was answered by Leila. She informed him that the items he wanted were in stock, but they were unable to deliver them, as the van was unavailable. Babic said he'll come around and pick up the order himself in about an hour. He emailed the list to her. After which he went to his van and fitted the dashboard camera from his car to the small delivery van. He switched it on and tested it. It was recording, he stopped it and played back. All was working well.

An hour later he pulled up in front of the clothing firm's premises, the dash cam was on. The marked DAF box van had gone, but the plain white one was parked out of the front. There were four men standing around the back of the van smoking. They seemed to be of Eastern Mediterranean appearance, lean and fit, almost like military. Babic angled the camera to face the back of the DAF, and the four guys grouped at the back of the vehicle. He got out and said to the men,

"As-salam'alaykum!" (Hello)

They repeated the greeting, and one of them said *"Hal tutakallam al-lughah al-arabujah?"* (Do you speak Arabic?)

Well, thought Babic these guys speak Arabic, he replied: *"Na'am qalilan,* (a little bit) but my first languages are English and Albanian. I learnt my Arabic at school and the mosque."

That seemed to relax them a bit, prior to that they had seemed somewhat sullen when he first arrived, but the greetings in what seemed to be the men's mother tongue broke the ice a bit. He went into the customer reception, and Leila was there already:

"Hi Afrim, we've got the order ready, but I need you to help me to bring it out."

"Where's Michael?"

"One of our vans is having its MoT done, he's taken it in. He should be back in an hour."

"No worries, but there are four hulking great blokes out there to help you."

"They are nothing to do with us, they seem to be friends of Mr Mashrani, they came yesterday. They are like Michael, Lebanese, but they don't like me having my head uncovered, I'm a Christian you see, like my colleague Michael. Anyway Afrim, let's not go there. Let's get you sorted out."

She led him into the main warehouse where there was a pallet trolley loaded with half a dozen cardboard boxes and a further half dozen on the floor beside it. Babic helped her to wheel the trolley out to his van, where she helped him load the back, they returned and brought out the remaining boxes. After the van was loaded, they returned to the office. The four men at the back of the van did not lift a finger to help. Their demeanour towards the young Syrian Christian was far from friendly. After Babic had collected the invoice he returned to his van, as he was about to get into the van one of the men said in heavily accented English: "How can you speak to a woman who fails to cover her head?"

"My brothers, you really need to be aware of our country's customs. We Muslims co-exist with our Christian, Hindu, Sikh and Jewish brothers and sisters. If you are going to settle here, you must be aware of this.

England on the whole is a kind, tolerant and good country. This is how we live."

"Well you are welcome to it; we won't be here for much longer."

"Ma'a as salamah!" (Goodbye!) said Babic, after which he drove off.

He made his way back to the shop. Where he uploaded the images from the dashcam onto his tablet. He dismantled the dash cam and re-mounted it back in his car. This done, he unloaded the van with the help of one of the shop assistants. He spent the next two hours unpacking the children's' clothing and setting it up on racks and shelving in the new section of the shop. He gave a price list to the assistant. She started to make up price tags, which she affixed to the items on the shelves and clothing racks. He went into the office and logged in to the system. He uploaded the new stock and its barcodes into the shops sales app. After this he composed an email to Pegg.

My dear friend,
I have to tell you that my decision to stock children's clothing was a good move. The first batch we purchased from Fashion Trends flew off the shelf so to speak. Today I visited Fashion Trends again and bought even more stock. Michael was not there. Leila told me that he had taken the marked van for its MoT. Mr Mashrani was not there either. But there were four new guys, who, Leila said had arrived yesterday. I asked Leila if they were new staff. She said no, she thought that they were friends of Mr Mashrani. She said they were, like Michael from Lebanon. I spoke with them, they spoke a bit of English, but they seemed to be very conservative Muslims, they did not like to see Leila without a head covering. I explained that in England this is what we do and get used to it. The guy I had spoken to said they were not here for long.

I'll let you know how well the clothing is selling. Regards Afrim.

* * *

Whilst Afrim Babic was restocking with clothing, Akbar Mashrani was touring eastern England. He was reconnoitring airfields. He had previously looked at Lincolnshire, and to that end had visited locations at Coningsby, Cranwell and Waddington. He had ruled them out as they were too public for his purposes. He was driving through Lincolnshire and heading into Norfolk. He had selected an airfield in the west of the county at Marham. He drove along a road which ran parallel to the main runway. Just after the village Fincham, he pulled in at the side of the road. He got out of the X5 and walked out onto a path on the edge of a field which had been sown with spring barley or wheat. There was a good view of the main runway, but there was no cover at all. There was clear line of sight both from and to the position he was stood at. A person standing in the field could be seen from anyone on the airfield, especially from a high observation point such as the control tower. To his right and behind him it was all open. He would try and see what the eastern end would offer.

He returned to the SUV and continued on the road. He passed a junction to his left but carried on past the turning. Looking to the left again the approach to the main runway was open fields. He drove on a bit further, before finding a place to turn around. He returned to the junction and turned right onto a road which passed by the eastern part of the airfield, to his left was the main part of the airfield He continued at about 15 mph; to the right were some auxiliary facilities, which may or may not have been part of the airfield. He could not see anywhere which would suit his purpose.

As he pondered these issues, he did not notice the airman with a dog, standing at the edge of an ammunition bunker, to his right. The airman spoke into his radio.

Unaware of this Mashrani continued driving; he came to a junction. The road ahead led to Narborough, the finger post indicating that the road to the left went Marham. He decided to turn the left turn. After about half a mile, there was another finger post. The sign had lettering which indicated "RAF Marham".

Mashrani turned left again and drove up the hill towards the airfield once more. He bore right around a bend and saw that the airfield was now to his left. The road straightened, he could see what appeared to be a housing estate ahead. He continued driving past the main gate of the air station. He had slowed down again to about 15 mph, maybe a bit too slowly. It was not long before he was being followed by an olive-green Land Rover.

Looking in his rear-view mirror, he saw that the vehicle flashed its headlights, the strobe beacons on its roof lighting bar were on.

Mashrani mouthed an oath, he had not meant to draw attention to himself. His cover was that he was trying to rustle up business for his wholesale clothing company. In the vehicle he had brochures and catalogues, as well as samples to back up his story. Reluctantly he pulled over. The Land Rover stopped behind his X5. An airman dressed in combat dress and wearing a flak jacket got out of the passenger side door and approached the driver's side of Mashrani's BMW SUV. The young man was of South Asian heritage, and was wearing corporals' chevrons on his shoulder slides, in addition he was wearing an arm band on his right sleeve, bearing the lettering "RAFP", there was a side arm in a holster which was strapped to his right hip. Mashrani did not see the body cam in the centre of the flak jacket.

"As-salam 'alaykan," the RAF policeman said. Before he could stop himself, he replied with the same Arabic greeting.

"So, you're a Muslim bruv?"

Mashrani cursed himself yet again. Not only had he drawn attention to himself, but the young airman had obviously looked at Mashrani's ethnicity, and guessed that Mashrani was a co-religionist, or it was some devious method of finding out a person's background.

"Like many in this country, yes I am a follower of the Prophet, peace be upon him."

"Thank you for stopping bruv, I need to take some details from you, just routine stuff, you know. You are in a restricted area; didn't you see the notice further back?"

Mashrani bristled at being addressed with such familiarity by a mere corporal, back in Iran he'd have had this underling severely dealt with for showing such disrespect to a senior officer. He pulled himself together, before answering:

"I saw no notice."

"Well it says that you are entering Ministry of Defence property, and that all personnel and their vehicles are liable to be stopped at any time. Please state your business." Mashrani wished he had taken more care. The trouble is people in this country just get on with their lives, unlike at home in Iran, you fart in the wrong place, and someone in authority will know about it. The apparent laissez-faire attitude of the Brits had lured him into a sense of false security. He had been arrogant in assuming he could carry on with his research without drawing attention to himself.

"I am so sorry I was looking for a shop. I am a businessman, a wholesaler who sells clothing to the retail trade."

"Well there are no clothing shops here, the nearest shop is in the village. You need to turn around and go back the way you came and follow the signs to Marham, you can't miss it it's on the right. But wait here a minute, whilst my colleague does some checks. Can I see your driving licence or some ID?"

Mashrani thought about arguing but decided it better that he comply with the airman's request. He produced a UK driving licence it was in his name, and the name on the licence would tally with the details held at DVLA. In addition, he produced a business card in the same name, with Fashion Trend's details printed underneath the name. "Just a minute, I'll go and have a word with my colleague."

The airman walked back to the Land Rover. He could see in the rear-view mirror, that the airman and his colleague were examining the document. One was on the radio, the other on a phone. A while later, the young airman returned, with the items Mashrani had given him.

"Thank you for your time bruv, you can be on your way, back there," he said indicating the direction Mashrani had come, he continued, "safe journey, *Ma' as salamah!*"

Mashrani loathed the way this upstart had been addressing him, he did not even acknowledge the farewell. He turned the X5 around and drove back the way he'd come without even a backward look. What's the matter with me he thought, I handled that so badly? He might as well have had a big sign above his head, "I'm an agent of the Guardians and I mean you harm." It was fortunate that the RAF policeman did not search his vehicle, they would have found the 1:25000 OS map of the area, with the annotations around the airfield area.

What Mashrani hadn't realised was that the air station was on heightened alert, as there had been an attempt to abduct an airman the previous week. A black SUV had pulled up beside an airman who had been jogging on the very road Mashrani had been driving on. The occupants of the SUV had tried to grab hold of the man, but being stronger and fitter than his potential abductors, he had managed to head-butt one of them, and kick another in the groin. After which he was able to sprint to safety. He had described his would-be abductors as either South Asian or Middle Eastern in appearance.

Mashrani was not suspected of anything else. But of course, he was not to know that. He continued away from the air base and headed towards Narborough and from there onto the A47, where he headed east, after a couple of miles, he pulled into a roadside rest area.

CHAPTER 15

Pegg was up early for his shift. Pat remained in bed; she was going to spend the day with Angie. He got into Dereham and was behind his desk by half past seven. Most of the night term officers were already back. He listened whilst the night shift sergeant briefed him as to the events of the previous night. There had been a couple of break-ins to shops in the town centre. A couple of suspects found on premises of the second of the break-ins were arrested and were currently in custody at the Wymondham Police Investigation Centre (WPIC). The arresting officers had made their statements, and copies had been emailed to the WPIC. Statements are needed from the shop managers. There were a couple of other things, a child had gone missing from a local care home, he was found earlier this morning. Follow up enquires needed to be made by Family Liaison. The other was some sheep rustling, Farm Watch has full details, could an officer go out to the farm this morning, and speak with both the farmer and the local Farm Watch rep.

At eight o'clock he was briefing the day shift, and twenty minutes later the officers were off to do their allotted tasks. Pegg returned to the sergeants' office. He checked his phone and saw that he had a new email from Babic. He read it. He then made a note of the salient points on a piece of paper which he placed in his messenger bag, together with Mo's file. He viewed the attached footage from Babic's dash cam. So now there are four unidentified Lebanese Arabs. Are these the "students" mentioned in the telephone messages between Pejman and the contact in Nottingham? He would obtain stills from the footage, at least he would have some faces to go on.

He put his phone away, and logged onto the Force intranet, from his workstation. He browsed through some intelligence reports about suspicious vehicles. His attention was drawn to an item put on recently. RAF Marham were on alert as there had been an attempt to abduct one of their airmen, by the occupants of a black SUV. As a result of this incident which had occurred last month, the RAF Police forwarded details of any sus vehicles, and their occupants   He clicked onto the report and opened it up. There were the details of black BMW X5, together with stills from the body cam footage of the RAF Police Corporal. Pegg looked in the file he had started after Mo's problems had begun. He checked the number of the BMW X5 which Babic had sent. It was the same. Well we have a connection with a military facility, thought Pegg. We'll have to follow the evidence and see where it leads us. Babic has seen and spoken to Mashrani, what needs to be done is to see if the driver whose face was recorded on the body cam is the same guy who Babic spoke with at Fashion Trends. He opened a still of the driver and printed it off. He placed the copy in Mo's file. After putting Mo's file back in his messenger bag, he printed off a copy of the RAF report and pinned it to the notice board in the briefing room.

Pegg was kept busy for the rest of the working day. Two of his officers were engaged in searching the houses of the two town centre burglary suspects. The searches had yielded evidence of other offences and a host of stolen property was recovered. This had resulted in the two miscreants being charged with further offences, and a lot of crimes were cleared up. Pegg drew a great deal of satisfaction, that it was uniformed officers who had done so much and made the job of the CID guys so much easier. He had a few rest days coming up, so he decided to clear his in tray. There were few crime files to sign off and get to the DS. He spent the rest of the shift finishing off various items of paperwork. By the time the shift had finished, he was ready for some down time, although he knew he would be far from relaxing for the next few days that he had off.

He drove back home.

* * *

Mashrani checked his phone, and found he had four bars, he'd get a good signal here. Before he made the call, he appraised his situation and how it may affect the planned mission. He had been compromised in his reconnaissance of Marham Airfield. He had been too overt in driving round. The air station must have some form of electronic surveillance around its perimeter and possibly beyond. He was confident that Shaqaz had not been telling tales to the authorities, the little queer knew what the penalty would be if he had opened his mouth. No, it must have been pure coincidence and bad luck that he had brought himself to the notice of the people at

Marham airfield. This is the time for some damage limitation, he would have to move the assets that he had gathered for the mission. It was with the greatest trepidation he picked up the phone and dialled the number.

"What is it?" asked Ali Mochta Ghazi, "I wasn't expecting you to call me so soon, are we ready for the job?"   "No, I have a problem, we will have to change the site of our enterprise, or even think about cancelling it altogether." Ghazi said nothing.

"Are you still there?" said Mashrani

"Of course I am, I'm thinking," said Ghazi. He paused again before continuing. "You realise that if this whole mission goes awry, all of us including Pejman, are likely to have nooses placed around our necks. So why are you saying we need to change?"

Mashrani explained what had happened, and that in order to get the changes under way he needed to contact Pejman. Mashrani continued:

"My first priority is to safeguard our merchandise, to that end I need to move it from its present location. At the moment it may be found by those who wish us harm."

"How so, it is away from prying eyes is it not?"

"It's not that, it's the fact that it could be, especially after the events at the airfield."

"So, what are you going to do about it?"

Mashrani explained that he would get the stuff loaded and transported to another, but just as secure location. He had to see about another mission. Ghazi said:

"Pejman will be in contact soon, meanwhile do as you suggest."

Mashrani made another call to Nottingham.

CHAPTER 16

Pegg got back home at four thirty. Pat's X-Trail was not there. He entered the house and changed out of his uniform and put on a pair of jeans and a sweatshirt. After which he took out his laptop and connected it to his printer/scanner.

He scanned the stills from the RAF Policeman's bodycam. Once this was done, he uploaded the scanned images.

He emailed Babic:

Afrim, thank you for your last email, I attach a couple of photos. Can you tell me if the guy in the picture is Mr Mashrani? Phone me as soon as you get this and delete this email in its entirety.

Many thanks Archie.

As he was packing away the laptop and printer, he heard a vehicle pulling into the driveway. Pat was back. The first one to the kitchen door was Fred, followed by Pat, who was laden with shopping bags.

"Well it seems that you have had a productive day," said Pegg, taking some of the bags off her.

"Yes, we had a great day, we ended up going to Norwich. Angie got some clothes for herself, and I bought some stuff for the baby, as well as for me."

She went on to explain how her day was spent. It was so nice to do clothes shopping in the company of a female friend. She showed him what she had bought; tops, woollen jerseys, shoes, and a couple of skirts.

"Very nice," said Pegg, "perhaps we can have a bit of a fashion show later, he continued, "Now what do you fancy to eat, or would you rather go out for our evening meal?"

"Could we eat in? I am a bit tired after our visit to The Fine City, I know I seem a bit boring."

"You boring, Pat, perish the thought."

"Oh Archie! You say the nicest things." She put har arms around him and rested her head against his chest, and then gave him a long, lingering kiss. They remained with their arms around each other, until Pat broke the moment, whispering into his ear:

"I need the bathroom, not very romantic, am I?" Pegg laughed and released her. She grabbed her bags and went upstairs. Pegg let Fred out into the garden. He decided to get on with the evening meal. He had some minced beef in the freezer. He decided on cottage pie, with peas and carrots. He defrosted the mince in the microwave, after which he started to peel some potatoes and carrots. That done, he cooked the now defrosted mince in a frying pan, adding tinned tomatoes and onion. Whilst he was doing this Pat came into the kitchen, she was wearing one of the skirts she had just bought, together with one of the tops and a pair of new shoes. She held the other skirt, and another of the tops in front of her.

"What do you think?" she asked.

"Wow! What a glamour puss, you look great in that!" Pat beamed and as she sniffed the odours emitting from the frying pan said:

"Mmm, Archie that smells delicious what are we having."

"Cottage pie, nothing too complicated but always a favourite. Now you need to go, I don't want the smell of cooking getting onto your newly purchased finery."

Pat laughed and went upstairs again. Pegg continued with cooking. Half an hour later he was mashing the potatoes, and after spreading the mash on the now cooked mince, which he had placed in a Pyrex dish. After placing the pie in the oven, he joined Pat who was sitting on the sofa after changing into a sweatshirt and jogging bottoms. He sat down and put his arm around her, she cosied up to him, resting her head on his shoulder. He told her about his day. And then the conversation moved onto them.

"Where do you see us in a years' time Pat?"

"I hope that we'll still be together, but at the moment we have separate lives and different jobs. I am happy with what we have got. Do you want more out of our relationship?"

"I can continue as we are, I do love you and I feel a very strong bond between us. Probably why we have such a deep friendship, is that we respect each other's space. The fact that we do not actually live with each other on a permanent basis does not mean that we can't be close. You are an independent person, and I respect that. So, as I have just said I am happy with what we've got." She turned her head and kissed him:

"Archie, I love you too, let's carry on as we are."

"Right Pat I need to see to our meal."

He got up and went back into the kitchen, he put the carrots and peas onto the stove, and turned the oven right down. He decided to eat in the kitchen, and to that end he laid the table out in the breakfast alcove. Pat came in.

"Anything I can do?"

"It's really all in hand, another 10 minutes and we eat. Perhaps you could get a bottle of wine from the garage, there's a nice Soave, which will go well with our meal."

"Of course, back in a minute."

She went out. Whilst she was out, Pegg's phone pinged it was an email from Afrim Babic:

Archie, in answer to your question. Yes that's the guy. Take care my friend. Afrim.

Pegg texted a brief acknowledgement. As he finished this, Pat returned with the bottle of wine. Pegg put the phone back on the work surface.

"Anything important?" she asked.

"Nothing that can't wait. Right Pat, can you see to the wine, there's a corkscrew in the cutlery tray. I'll sort out the vegetables."

A short while later they were sitting down and enjoying their meal. The conversation turned to what they would do the next day. Pegg suggested that they spend a day up in North Norfolk, he had thought of going to Norwich, but as Pat had already been up there today, there was no point.

"We'll go up to Wells-next-Sea and do a bit of the coastal walk. Not quite as hilly as the Peaks and Dales, but just as lovely."

"Sounds great. Let's do it!"

Pegg was aware that his commitment to Mo's problems could well impinge on Pat's visit. He decided to let her know what he was doing. She was well aware of his previous endeavour when he helped an old army friend to clear his name of spurious allegations of war crimes.

"Pat there is something I have to tell you, but it is in the strictest confidence, as people's wellbeing could be at stake, if what I am about to inform you gets out. It is only fair that you are in the know, as I may have to change our plans, regarding our time together for the next couple of weeks."

"I'm fine with that. If need be, I can cut my visit short."

"You'll do no such thing Pat Warrington! I want your company!"

"Well if there is anything I can do to help…."

"Be careful what you say, I'll probably take you up on that!" Pegg interrupted.

He went onto explain what had happened to Mo in Iran, and how he had fled the country and eventually made a life for himself here in the UK. And finally to his current predicament. Pegg went onto say:

"What I have found out is that Mo is being coerced to helping a bunch of really bad guys to carry out some serious and damaging stuff. One of the main players is a chap called Akbar Mashrani, he manages a wholesale clothing company in Nottingham, but I have reason to believe that he is operating as an undercover illegal; he is in fact a colonel in the Quds Force, an elite section of the Iranian Revolutionary Guards Corps.

'I have also found out that he is in league with an Ali Mochta Ghazi, the Agricultural Attaché at the Iranian Embassy in London. He is also an officer in the IRGC Quds Force. I have proof that Mashrani has been snooping around the RAF base at Marham. There is still a lot to do. Mo has been told to make a storage facility available to Mashrani, and I am waiting for Mo to let me know when that will be."

"Any idea what sort of stuff these people want to put in Mo's storage unit?" she asked.

"That's the 64-million-dollar question. When they start putting the stuff in there, I'll be taking a look at it."

"Well remember my background, I've got a very wide and diverse knowledge of technical stuff. So if you need some help in identifying items of kit, I'm your woman."

"I may be taking you up on that!"

They'd finished their meal, and after clearing and washing up, they returned to the living room. Pegg put on some music and joined Pat on the sofa. He put his arm around her, and she rested her head on his chest. They remained like that, listening to the Mozart's beautiful clarinet concerto.

"Archie, love, I wish that we could stay like this forever."

"Me too," he said, kissing the top of her head.

CHAPTER 17

At Fashion Trends the phone rang Leila picked up the phone.

"Leila, Mashrani here, I want you to close up for the rest of the day."

"We are expecting a couple of clients later."

"I don't care, tell them to come back tomorrow."

"But Mr Mashrani......."

"Do as you are told girl, you and Michael take the rest of the day off, now!" Mashrani terminated the call.

He made a further call to the phone he had given to one of the Lebanese visitors, the conversation was in Arabic: "Yusef we have a problem, I am on my way back to Nottingham, I'll phone you again when I get there. Meanwhile I want you guys to pack up your stuff, we'll not be coming back to the guest house."

Mashrani ended the call and started the journey back to Nottingham. On the way he was thinking of his options. He did not know if his run-in with the RAF Police at Marham would result in Fashion Trend's premises being put under surveillance, or even worse being raided. He still had the industrial unit in Reydon, near Southwold, Suffolk. He would get the stuff moved to there, out of the way of prying eyes. He had to be sure that his assets were secure until they were ready for use. He now had to revise his current plans. The events at Marham had shown that his plans for this chosen airfield were well and truly dead in the water.   Once the removal of the assets had been completed, he could turn his hand in seeking another location where the operation can be successfully executed. He continued driving and eventually was pulling up in front of Fashion Trends. After parking up the X5, he went to the office entrance door, and using his own set of keys, gained access to the now vacant premises.

He used the office phone to contact the Lebanese visitors, speaking Arabic he said:

"Yusef get yourself and the others down to Fashion Trends as soon as you can. You'll not be staying in Nottingham anymore. I am going to arrange alternative accommodation."

He ended the call and switched on one of the office's desktop computers. He went online and searched for caravan parks near to the industrial estate at Reydon. He found a couple which would fit the bill. The first one was in Southwold itself, near to the pier. He tried the number. Yes they had a static caravan available, sleeps six persons. Mashrani asked if he could rent it for two weeks. The site owner was more than happy with this. Not too many people were holidaying at that time of year. Mashrani used his company card to pay for the two weeks. The site owner said the office closes at six in the evening, but guests arriving after hours can still obtain the keys to their static. They had a facility by which the keys would be available. There is a safe outside the site office, he gave Mashrani the numbers to the safe's keypad. The number of the static would be on the keys tag. Next he phoned Leila, again he spoke Arabic: "Leila, I shall be away for the next few days, I will be using the plain white DAF van, the Polo, and one of the Ford vans, it will be the green one. You and Michael can use the X5 whilst I am away. That together with the other two vans should be enough for your needs."

"When will you be back?"

"I can't say, but I want you and Michael to continue to run the business. You are both very competent, and I have every confidence you'll do a good job. I will leave Fashion Trends in your capable hands." He ended the call.

Later the green Ford Connect van pulled up outside, followed by the blue VW Polo a couple of minutes after it.

The four Lebanese walked in, carrying the bags they had when they arrived in England. Mashrani handed the keys to the white DAF to one of the Lebanese, and after the main roller door was opened, the man reversed the DAF into the warehouse. This done, the door was shut again. The next two hours were spent packing large cardboard crates, two dozen in number. The crates were loaded onto the DAF.

Four hours after Mashrani had arrived in Nottingham, three vehicles left the industrial estate, heading towards Suffolk.

CHAPTER 18

The following day Pegg and Pat were up and about by 8 o'clock. They had breakfast, were getting ready for their trip out to the North Norfolk coast. Pegg decided to take his Land Rover. He said to Pat:

"I need to make a phone call before we go, it's to do with the thing I'm doing for Mo."

"No problem Archie, do you want me out of the way?"

"Of course not!"

Pegg used his mobile to call Manchester.

"Open Justice Advocates, how may we help? "

"It's Archie Pegg here, can you put me through to Samuel

Davidson."

Samuel Davidson was one of the senior partners of OJA, Rachel Gluckstein being the other. The firm had been a major player in Pegg's quest for justice for his old comrade Tony Spratt. Sam was also an expert on Israel, its politics, people, and its security services, and the Israeli Defence Forces (IDF). He had written many articles and books on the subject.

A short while after, he was put through to Davidson:

"Archie how can we help?"

"Sam it's a delicate one. I have been helping a friend who is in a great deal of trouble."

"Not another veteran? You helped us to wind up that dreadful Balkans War Crimes Team."

"No Sam, this is not to do with any veteran, this is to do with an Iranian guy, who is actually a very successful businessman here in the UK. He's a British citizen now. Without going into too much detail, the Islamic Republic is threatening his family in Iran, if he does not help them in what I must assume is some nefarious activity."

"I see so what do you want me to do?"

"I've done quite a bit of research into this situation, and the portents do not look too good. There are some bad guys out there on the loose, and I am trying to put names to faces. I have some dash cam footage of four guys, they are apparently Lebanese. The quality of the video is good. If I send you the video can you help me out."

"I can't Archie, but I know some people who might be able to help."

"You can? Oh Sam you are a lifesaver. If I email you a dash cam video, do you think someone could ID the four guys?

"I'll see what I can do. Is this official?

"Not yet, I'm working under the radar, and lives are at stake if the authorities are made aware at this stage. Have you got a private email; I think it's better not to go through OJA's inbox?"

"I'll see what I can do for you here's my own email address."

Pegg wrote it down. He then sent an email to it, attaching the video from Babic's dash cam footage.

"Right Pat let's go."

After securing the house, and closing the front gate, Pegg drove off. They headed north on the B1146 to Fakenham, from there they drove onto the B1105 and finally to Wells-next-the-Sea. Pegg found a slot on the quay's car park. When he had parked up he said: "We'll head up to the beach. It's about a mile from here. You've got a choice Pat. We can either take the Wells Harbour Light Railway, or we can walk up Beach Road."

"We'll walk Archie."

They walked up Beach Road towards the Lifeboat Station. The road was straight and flat. The sun had come out, and the wind had got up. The tide was coming in, and the mud flats to their right were now covered by the rising water, the surface of which was being whipped up into wavelets by the strengthening wind. Their immediate destination, the Lifeboat Station, was hidden from view by the dunes and trees, which ran in a continuous line left from the water as far as the eye could see.

When they reached the end of Beach Road, Pegg let Fred off his lease, and they made way up over the dune and to the Lifeboat Station.

"How long have they had a lifeboat here, Archie?

"Well from what I remember, there has been some sort of lifeboat here since 1830. I believe the RNLI took over the responsibility for sea rescue in 1869. There has been a continued RNLI presence here since."

"What sort of boats do they use?"

"They currently have an all-weather boat, which has a crew of six, and also a light inshore boat, which is crewed by three to four. I know you'll say how do I know this, well one of my old army mates is a RNLI crewman. He is always waxing lyrical about the organisation, and what type of boat is stationed where around the RNLI's stations along the Norfolk coast. He's proud of what he does, they do such a wonderful job; so I do not hold it against him if he is a bit of an "anorak" so to speak."

They walked around the station looking at the various plaques and photographs, and after putting some money in the collection box, they left continuing to follow the westbound Norfolk Coastal Path. The sea was on their right and the Holkham Nature Reserve marshes were on their left.

"You know Archie, up in the peaks we have the hills and moors, but her in flat East Anglia, and especially Norfolk, you have huge open skies. It gives such a feeling of wide space."

"It does really, and the picture changes on a daily and even hourly basis." Pegg replied. He continued, "We'll walk to Holkham and perhaps we can get a meal at the pub there."

"Sounds good," said Pat.

106

They continued onto Holkham, and after reaching Holkham Gap, they walked along the straight Lady Ann's Road towards Holkham Hall. After a 5 mile walk they reached their destination. Unfortunately for them, dogs were not allowed in the pub, and they were too late for a meal.

"I'll tell you what Pat, let's get the bus back to Wells, there is an excellent fish shop on the Quay." He looked at his watch, "there should be one soon."

"Let's do it, "she said.

They made their way to the bus stop, which was on the other side of the from the pub. Ten minutes later, the bus arrived, and they boarded it for the fifteen-minute journey back to Wells. The bus stopped at the Quay, where they alighted. They went back to the Land Rover, Pegg gave Fred a drink.

He asked Pat:

"Do want to eat in the Lanny and look over the harbour or eat indoors."

"Oh let's eat out, there's a lot to see."

After putting Fred in the back of the Land Rover, they made their way to the fish and chip shop. They both ordered cod and chips. Pegg explained that the fish bar had a reputation for being the best in this part of Norfolk.

"I can't wait for mine, I'm famished, "said Pat.

"That makes two of us then!" replied Pegg. Once they got their food, they crossed the road and returned to the Land Rover where they ate their meal. When they had finished eating, Pegg gathered up the detritus, and deposited it in a nearby litter bin.

"You weren't wrong about the food Archie, that's the best fish I've had in a long time," said Pat.

They sat and talked, Fred had, meanwhile joined them, and was sitting between them both.

Pegg's phoned pinged. It was a text from a person who just calls himself Simon.

WHEN YOU GET THIS, CALL ME FROM A LAND LINE IMMEDIATELY. IT IS A MATTER OF UTMOST URGENCY. WHEN YOU HAVE CALLED DELETE THIS STRAIGHT AWAY. IT'S ABOUT YOUR CALL TO SAM. SIMON.

"Oops Pat, you know that call I made to the solicitor in Manchester?"

"The one you made before we went out this morning?"
"That's the one, well it seems I've got to return the call by landline. Give me a couple of minutes, while I find a call box, and return the guy's call."

"That's fine I need to use the loo, I'll go to the one in the Fish and Chip Shop."

Pegg got out, while Pat made her way to the Fish and Chip shop. He had secured the Land Rover, with Fred inside, and had given the keys to Pat. He could not find a public call box, but he found a public phone at the Bowling Green Inn, in Church Street.

He put his money in the box and called the mobile number. The call was answered:

"Hello."

"Hello, it's Archie Pegg, can I speak to Simon?"

"Speaking, hang up now and I'll get straight back to you."   A minute later the phone rang again. Pegg picked up.

"Mr Pegg, it's Simon, thank you for your time. Samuel Davidson sent us the footage of your friend's dash cam. We checked with our colleagues on their data base. It seems that your friend has got some pictures of some really bad guys. I need to talk to you in person as soon as I can."

"Who are you Simon and who do you work for?"
"Who I am and who I work for, you do not need to know at this stage. But I can assure you that you are speaking

to one who is a friend, and whose people mean you no harm at all. Now where are you at the moment?"

"I'm currently at a seaside town in North Norfolk, Wellsnext-the-Sea."

"That's where you live?"

"No I live in Mid Norfolk about 28 miles away." "I really need to talk to you, I am about a couple of hours away, can I see you today, at home?"

"I suppose so," Pegg gave him his home address and postcode.

"I shall leave within the hour and I'll text you when I leave. Talk later, goodbye Mr Pegg.

Pegg left the pub and made his way back to the Quay. Pat was already sitting in the Land Rover, with Fred on her lap.

"Sorry for being so long, I could not find a public call box, so I ended going to a pub and using theirs."

"That's okay, did you get it sorted out?"

"Not really, the guy I called wants to see me in person, I've agreed to see him today, at home. It seems that the guys who Afrim filmed on his dash cam are some really bad 'uns."

"Gosh Archie, I can't say that it's boring being with you! So what do you want me to do, stay out of the way?"

"No I want you to be with me if you don't mind. Your input would be useful, anyway you are part of this. You okay with that?"

"Of course come on let's go back and find out what all this is about."

They left the Quay and drove out of the town and headed south back to Fakenham, and from there back to Gressenhall, arriving back at Pegg's house some forty minutes later. After Pegg had parked up, and they had taken their stuff from the Land Rover into the house, they sat down in the living room with a mug of tea each.

"Thanks for a lovely day out, Archie. Gosh that sea breeze

really does clean out the lungs," said Pat as she sipped her tea.

"My pleasure sweetheart, I enjoyed it as well. Pity about the pub lunch, I should have done a bit more research."

"The takeout from the fish bar more than made up for it. I shan't need much more to eat today, that was really filling." They talked about their day. As they were talking Pegg's mobile pinged. He saw that it was a text from Simon:

ON A10 JUST PASSED THROUGH WATERBEACH, BE WITH YOU IN AN HOUR OR SO. SIMON

"Right Pat I've a feeling we may be in for a late night"

"We'll have to wait and see how the evening pans out."

CHAPTER 19

Around the same time that Pegg and Pat were waiting for the mysterious Simon. The small convoy which had left Nottingham arrived at the industrial estate on the edge of Reydon in Suffolk.

The DAF was reversed up to the main door of the unit. Mashrani unlocked the side door, and a couple of minutes later the main roller door was open. The DAF again reversed, this time into the unit, and the roller door was closed again.

Speaking in Arabic Mashrani addressed the four Lebanese, who had by this time joined Mashrani in the unit:

"Right my brothers, we have to remain here for a little bit. I will contact you soon in order to brief you on our mission. Due to circumstances which you do not need to know about, I have to do a bit more research. Now this has made it necessary for us to move out of Nottingham. Your temporary accommodation is about a mile down the road.

I'll take you down there after I have finished speaking with you.'

"The DAF and the Ford van will remain with you here. Use the van but leave the DAF here in the unit. I do not want it unloading at the moment. Yusef I want one person here in the unit at all times. That person is to remain in the building and not venture outside. Keep all the doors locked, and only open it for one of you. I leave it to you to work out the shifts'

'Make sure you let the person in the unit know when any or all of you are coming up. I want movement to and from the unit kept to a minimum. Only come up when there is a shift change. Are your weapons available Yusef?"   "We have the Glocks available for immediate use. The M16s are still packed away in the back of the DAF."   "Right you will only use firearms as a last resort. Keep the pistols out of sight at all times. We must not compromise our mission. One of you who is staying behind, make sure that your phone is on vibrate only. Lock up when we go.

Yusef will arrange for you to be relieved later. The rest of you in the van and follow me. I'll take you to your accommodation."

Ten minutes later Mashrani had parked outside the static, having obtained the keys from the safe outside the now closed site office. He briefed the three Hezbollah fighters, where they could shop for supplies and food. He recommended the Co-op store in Southwold High Street which was about a ten-minute walk away.

Mashrani left the Lebanese and drove back to Norfolk. He booked into a hotel near the Royal Norfolk Showground, which was located about a couple of miles from Norwich City Centre. He fetched his luggage and briefcase from the Polo, and went to his room, where he got out his laptop, and the OS maps he had with him, when he was stopped at Marham airfield.

He logged into his laptop and using the hotel's Wi-Fi commenced to do a search of local military airfields. There were three in Suffolk, and two in Norfolk. He had ruled out Marham, so his attention was drawn to North Wendlesham. He brought up the webpage and saw that it was a United States Air Force base, and that it was even nearer to Dereham than the airfield at Marham. He found the location of the American facility on the OS map. In the morning he would drive there and carry out a reconnaissance of the area, after which he would call Ghazi who would in turn contact Pejman. Hopefully Mashrani believed he would get approval for the change in the mission from that he had originally planned. It would be even better now, as the Great Satan, and not the Little Satan would be the subject of the new operation.

CHAPTER 20

Back in Gressenhall, the doorbell rang at Pegg's house. Fred barked and ran to the front door. Pegg switched on the outside light and picking the dog up, opened the door. A tall proportionally built man dressed in a navy-blue overcoat, and wearing a matching flat cap stood outside on the front doorstep. He was carrying a black messenger bag.

"Hello Mr Pegg, I'm Simon." He held his right hand out and Pegg took it.

"Simon, nice to see you, come in. Where's your car?"

"I left it parked near the shop," he replied, stepping into the hallway.

"That'll be okay there." Pegg closed the door, and put down the wriggling poodle, who sniffed around Simon legs.

Simon tickled his ears. "Let me take your hat and coat." Simon took off his overcoat and hat to reveal he was wearing a sweatshirt, and blue corduroy trousers. Pegg took the hat and coat and hung them on a spare hook on the hallway's coat rack.

Pegg ushered Simon into the living room. Pat was sitting down, Fred leapt onto her lap and stared intently at Simon, who froze when he saw Pat.

"Chaim Eban, as I stand and breathe. Well I never!" she exclaimed.

Simon/Chaim said nothing. Pegg finally broke the silence:

"Am I missing something here? Will somebody tell me what the heck is occurring?"

"Sorry Archie, I met Chaim at the renewables symposium at the UEA, in Norwich last year. You remember I was with Sheffield University's research group. We were demonstrating our new design for a cylindrical wind turbine."

"That's right Mr Pegg, I was wearing my hat as a visiting lecturer in renewable energy technology. We were very impressed with Miss Warrington's team and their ideas."

"Well Chaim, or whoever you are, I'm Archie and this lady is my girlfriend Pat. As it appears that we will be working together we need to be able to trust each other. So let's have a bit of background about you and your interest in our friend Mohammed Shaqaz's situation."   "May I?" asked Eban indicating to a vacant armchair. Pegg nodded, and Eban sat down. He continued, "I really am an academic, and I work as a visiting lecturer. I am currently at Cambridge, a temporary post, but one in which I will be for the next six months. I cannot tell you who my official paymasters are, but I will say that they are friendly towards your country." He paused before continuing, "We are very concerned about the activities of certain Iranians, who are working as illegals on behalf of the Iranian Revolutionary Guards Corps. We believe a section of their Quds Force has gone rogue, and maybe operating without the knowledge of the Islamic Republic's leadership. It would help my people if you could tell me what you know. Samuel Davidson forwarded some footage from a dash cam, which has really got alarm bells ringing."

"That footage was filmed in Nottingham," said Pegg. "It was filmed outside the premises of Fashion Trends, a clothing wholesale supplier. The manager is a guy, an Iranian called Akbar Mashrani."

"Mashrani is a high-ranking officer in Quds Force. He has been working under cover for the past four years. He came to the UK under the guise of an asylum seeker. Apparently he has been given leave to stay indefinitely."

"How do these people slip under the radar of our intelligence services?" asked Pegg.

"Quite frankly, the system is overloaded and just can't cope with the volume of people claiming asylum. Most of the asylum seekers who come to Britain are genuine and are in real danger in their homelands. You can see how easy it is for the occasional bad apple to slip in," said Eban.   "So where do we go from here?" asked Pegg.

"Well I'm here to help you with what information I can. Why have you not been and reported all the stuff which you have to Special Branch for example?"

Pegg explained the reason they were keeping what they had found out to themselves. How Mo had been coerced into making his premises available for Mashrani's nefarious activities. The threat to his parent's welfare being the price he would pay if he refused to help them.

"What if his parents were taken out of danger, how would Mo react to that?"

"That's something I have not even thought about. But I expect that this would put a completely different light on things."

"Okay let's leave this for a bit. We will compare what we have got so far."

Pegg got up and said, "I suggest that we go into the kitchen and sit around the table in the dining area." They got up and made their way to the table, Pegg taking his file and Eban his messenger bag. He took out a Mac Book and set it up in front and sat down. Pegg sat in the place next to Eban, whilst Pat drew up a chair and sat beside him. Pegg opened his file with the accumulated notes, printouts, and photos. He went through everything he had done since he had his first meeting with Mo up to the time he had contacted Sam Davidson. He had reservations about breaking his pledge to keep things confidential between Mo and himself. Since making that pledge he had confided in Pat and now Chaim Eban. But if there was a chance of getting Mo's mum and dad to a safe place, maybe it is a price worth paying.

"Right," said Eban, "let me show you what I have got for you. When we got the dash cam footage Sam sent us, we searched our data bases, and on scrolling through our records regarding Shia militias in Lebanon, we matched all the faces in the footage to some of the top stars among the Hezbollah fighters. They all come from Beirut and we have put names to faces.'

'First is Yusef-al-Haddad, he's the tallest of the four, he used to be a very good wrestler, Olympic standard, I'd say, although we have no record of him competing in any games. He is a veteran of fighting in Iraq and Syria. We should not underestimate him.'

'Standing on Yusef's right is another veteran of Iraq and Syria he's Ahmad-bin-Khoury. This is the first time that we have seen him with Yusef. He has also been involved in hostage taking, and we think people trafficking as well. Not a very nice guy.'

'On Yusef's left is someone we do not have much information about, our sources believe he is called Kaled Hariri.'

'The last guy, who is standing on the right of the group next to Ahmad is Naji-bin-Azzi. He is a particularly nasty piece of work. He deals drugs, engages in sectarian murders, both of Sunni Muslims and Christians. I'm really surprised he'd be used in specialist operations outside of Beirut."

Pegg noted down the names of the four Hezbollah militia men and made notes against each of their names. "Mashrani is going to use these guys in some form of operation, it will be a Quds Force affair, these militia men are being used as surrogates. They obviously have some kit which Mashrani does not want people outside this little group to know about. His own employees at Fashion Trends were never allowed near the stuff. Probably as well, because from what we know about these people they would not hesitate in killing innocents who stumbled across what they were doing. It goes without saying they will be armed, so utmost caution will be needed if we go near them. But having said that, they would not want to draw attention to themselves."

"So how are we going to deal with this?" asked Pat.

"I think we need a free hand. We need to get Mo on side. The way we do that is to get his parents out of the way of Pejman. In my view this can be done in one of two ways; either they are moved to a place of safety in Iran, or we bring them out and into Mo's care."

"How on earth can we do that?" she said.

"Yes that seems like mission impossible to me," added Pegg.

"There are people who can facilitate the extraction of personnel out of Iran and other places in the Middle East, believe you me. I am not prepared to say how, but it can be done, as it's done on an almost daily basis. Now do you
want to get this done or not?"

"Well Chaim it's not for us to say, I think we need to talk with Mo." When would it be best to do this?"   Chaim said nothing. Eventually he said:

"Can you call him now?"

Pegg rang Mo. Esi answered the call:

"Archie how is it going?"

"We're fine, is it possible to speak to Mo? It's quite important."

Esi put down the phone and few moments Mo came on the line.

"Hello Archie, I still have not heard that number. What is it that's so important that you want to call me at this time of the evening?"

"Mo I'll cut right to the chase. There may be a way of getting your mum and dad out of harm's way. I can't explain how at the moment, but I may be able to put you in touch with people who can arrange this."

"You are kidding me Archie, it would be wonderful if you could, but I'll not be holding my breath."

"If it could be arranged, would you still carry on with letting your storage facility in Dereham being used. It would help us nail these bastards if you could."

"You get my parents to safety and I'll do whatever it takes to help."

"Can you be ready to speak to somebody within the next few minutes or so Mo?"

"I'll do that, speak soon."

Pegg ended the call. Eban wrote down Mo's number and said:

"Do you mind if I speak to Mo privately? I'll use my own phone."

"Of course, we'll go into the living room."

Pat and Pegg left the kitchen, closing the door behind them. They sat down on the sofa. Fred again sat on Pat's lap.

"Well I seem to have got you involved in something that maybe I shouldn't have done, "said Pegg.

"It's never dull being with you Archie I must say! I really only knew Chaim from the time we were at the UEA last year. Who do you think he really is?"

"I have my suspicions, but I do not want to speculate too much."

"Who do you think he is working for?"

"From the way things are looking, he could be some sort of intelligence operative."

"You mean some sort of spy?"

"Yes something like that. If he is he's working under the radar of our people. That being the case we need to keep this between ourselves. Are you still in with me on this?"

"Of course."

"All the way, come whatever?"

"One hundred per cent."

They sat and talked. Fifteen minutes later Eban knocked on the living room door and came in.

"Right I've got to go to Norwich and see Mo. There are a couple of things I need to give him."

"Are you going right away? Do you want something to eat?" asked Pegg.

"I need to leave right now. I will give you a burner phone, it has my contact details. Call me any time day or night if you have any more information. I cannot stress strongly enough that what went on this evening must stay between us. That way we'll remain safe. We are dealing with some very unpleasant and dangerous people."

He went back to the kitchen and took a mobile phone out of his messenger bag and gave it to Pegg. Pegg fetched his hat and coat and Eban put them on.

"Take care the both of you, I'll be in touch." He gave Pat a kiss on each cheek and shook Pegg's hand. Pegg opened the front door, and Eban disappeared into the night.

"Well this is going faster than I thought. When do you have to be back in Sheffield as I may need you to help me out? I can't go to any official agency about this situation we find ourselves in."

"I'm alright for the next week or so. The department have my contact details, so they'll call if they need me. I'm going to have a shower, care to join me?"

"That sounds like a plan, let's do it!"

CHAPTER 21

The following day Major Tom O'Brien was at the controls of his F15 Eagle, he was approaching the 09 threshold of the main runway at North Wendlesham. In the backseat of the aircraft was his Weapons Systems Officer (WSO), which in service parlance was also known as a "Wizzo". He rolled the jet onto the threshold and waited for the second aircraft, his wingman to pull up alongside. They were on a training flight to north of the country, where they would be visiting a range, to practice bomb runs. The weather was fair, cloud cover was around 2000 feet, and visibility was good. The Met Report stated that there was no precipitation either on their planned course nor over the target area and winds were north westerly, with wind speeds of twenty to thirty knots; all in all, good weather for flying, not that mattered a great deal to the type aircraft he was flying.

There had been a lot on O'Brien's mind. His main cause of concern was the future of the Posetti twins. It had transpired that there were no family members suitable to take on the two orphans. His wife June was looking after them for the time being. The toddlers were doing well after the trauma they had suffered in the car crash which claimed the lives of their parents. Both he and June adored having them, but at some stage they would have to hand them over to some agency for adoption. He had discussed it with June; they would like to put their names forward as adoptive parents. They were relatively young, he being forty-five and June was forty-three. His son was twenty-one and was in his first year of a law degree at Boston University, whilst his daughter of seventeen was in her last year at college also at Boston.

She lived with O'Brien's parents, whilst in the States, coming back to North Wendlesham during the school holidays. It would break both his and June's hearts if the children were taken away from them.

As he waited for clearance to take off, he glanced briefly at a car park to his right, beyond the perimeter fence. There were a few cars parked there. He did not notice the blue VW Polo parked amongst them. The control tower gave clearance for take-off. O'Brien pushed the throttle levers forward through the gate, and the Pratt & Whitney FV100 turbofans roared to full power. The jet sped down the runway, with the second aircraft following suit, seconds later they were in the air, banking to starboard and heading north.

*   *   *

Akbar Mashrani had parked up in an area which had been designated as an unofficial viewing area. It was located at the eastern end of North Wendlesham airfield. He was not alone, there were a dozen assorted vehicles parked there as well, including a burger van. Some of the vehicles' occupants were standing at the edge of the parking area, which was adjacent to the airfield's perimeter fence.

This suited Mashrani, he could observe the aircraft movements without drawing unwanted attention to himself. In this part of the country the prevailing winds were westerlies. At this particular airfield along with many in the United Kingdom, aircraft would land and take off into the wind. On this particular day he had observed over the past hour about twenty jets taxiing to the 09 threshold and taking off. All of the aircraft had engaged their engines' afterburners when taking off. Mashrani was not a trained airman, but he assumed that this procedure was necessary if the aircraft were carrying a full load of stores and fuel.   Whatever the reason was, a large heat source was being generated out of the back of the aircraft. He had witnessed a pair of jets landing, on this occasion there was no reheat, and the whole procedure was much quieter. The aircraft probably did not have any stores on board and the fuel load would have been much less. He decided to have a look at the western end of the airfield. He had identified an area where he could park on the 1/50000 OS map he had on his lap. He put the map back into the glove compartment and drove out of the parking area.

He passed through North Wendlesham village, stopping at a lay-by, about a mile to the west of the village. He got the OS map out again, after studying it again, he folded it up and put it in a map case. He got out of the car, opened the tailgate, and retrieved a Helly-Hansen jacket and a rucksack. After putting on the jacket, he eased the straps of the ruck sack over his shoulders, finally he put a black beanie hat on his head, pulling the sides down over his ears. He was glad of it as there was a cold north westerly wind blowing. He checked himself in the car's wing mirror. Just like any other person out on a countryside ramble, he thought to himself.

There was a public footpath leading out of the lay-by, up a slight hill towards a wooded area, on either side of the track there was a hedgerow, which consisted of a mixture of hawthorn and blackthorn. The foliage was just starting to show on the hawthorn. In a month or so it would be out fully, together with the sweet-smelling Mayflower. Mashrani was not interested in the flora of the Norfolk countryside, but he was glad that the footpath was out of sight from the road on which he had just driven. He continued up towards the wooded area which in point of fact was a small forest, with a variety of trees, mainly beech and oak, but also some pines. His attention was drawn to the sound of jet engines, he glanced to his left and saw four F15 Eagles climbing into the air. The 27 threshold at the western end of the airfield's runway was about half a mile away. The jets roared overhead, banking away to starboard and heading north.   From where he was standing the whole airfield was spread out before him. He walked on. Where the wood ended the footpath continued on over open fields. The hedgerow on the left of the footpath continued but the right hand one petered out after a couple of hundred metres. After about half a mile, the path ran downhill, and the airfield was lost from view. At the bottom of the hill the path ran past a concrete hard standing, on which was piled harvested sugar beet.

There was a tractor and trailer, parked beside and a front loader was busy loading up the trailer. The operator of the front loader ignored Mashrani, continuing with his task of loading the trailer. The hard standing was situated adjacent to a road, one of the myriads of narrow lanes which crisscrossed the county. Mashrani looked at his map and found the location of the beet pad. The lane next to the beet pad ran north to south. The map showed that if he turned right onto the road and continued along it, he would come to a junction after a mile, turning right again at the junction would eventually take him back to where he had parked his car. He was still, contemplating the situation, when he heard the tractor starting up, and pulling the trailer off the beet pad, and onto the lane. This time the loader operator was now driving the tractor. The tractor and its load headed south along the lane. Mashrani decided to walk back the way he had come. When he got back to the small forest, he took a notebook out of his rucksack, and made a rough sketch of the area. After completing this he resumed and ten minutes later he was back in his car. He drove out of the area and towards Suffolk and Southwold.

CHAPTER 22

In Iran, Darius and Muna Shaqaz, Mo's parents, had left their small flat. They were doing some food shopping in their local market. They had not been directly harassed by Pejman's operatives, but a shadow followed them. On this particular day, the Guardian who was tasked to watch the couple was thoroughly bored, he had been doing the same job for the past month. He had been told he would not have to do this for much longer, as the couple's usefulness will soon be over. The Guardian was paying more attention to games on his phone, than to the immediate job in hand. Darius and Muna, meanwhile were browsing at a fruit and vegetable stall. Darius was haggling over the price of some mangoes. His wife was behind him. A stooped figure dressed in the long black robes that were vestments de rigeur among the women in the Islamic Republic, stood beside Muna, whist eying the produce on display. The male voice from under the black clothing whispered in English: "Act normally do not look at me, I have a message from your son."

An envelope was thrust into her hand and the bearer was gone before Muna had a chance to react. She was hard put to conceal her surprise and at the same time her delight. She thrust the envelope into her shopping bag, covering it up with some tins of food she had already purchased. Darius had agreed a price for the mangoes, and after paying for them and the other fruit and vegetables the items were placed in the bag on top of the tins and the envelope.   The remittances which Mo sent them were the only source of income they had. They were not able to work, as Pejman had made sure that they were blacklisted as far as working in schools was concerned. Even the small job Muna had as a librarian had been terminated; Darius was not even able to carry on as a cleaner in one of the schools in the town. After visiting a couple of more shops they walked back home. The Guardian managed to drag himself away from his phone, he put the device away and followed them back to their flat. He reported back to his supervisor, who stood him down. Their informant in the block of flats where Darius and Muna lived would let the Guardians know if the couple went out again, and in addition there was the listening device in the small living room. Unknown to the Guardians, Darius, had located the device. It was seated within a small recess which housed a ventilator. He decided to leave it alone. Any confidential conversations were carried out in the kitchen or bathroom. When Darius and Muna got back to their flat, Muna beckoned Darius and they went into the kitchen, where Muna switched on the radio, which was playing some religious music. She told him about the strange "woman" and the envelope which she was given. She opened it and read the letter inside. The letter was in English, a language which both these former teachers spoke and read.

"Dear Mama and Papa,
The bearer of this letter is a friend. He and others will assist you to leave and join me in England. You are both in extreme danger if you remain in Iran. Tomorrow go shopping as normal. Go to the same market. Walk through the market and enter a small emporium, there is a clothing shop the second shop on the right as you enter. Go in there and ask to use the toilets. There is a back door which leads into a small side street. You will find a grey van parked there, the people in the van will drive you away. Do not take anything with you except your passports and your shopping bags. Papa, take your medication with you. I will see you soon. God go with you. I love you always.
Mohammed

PS Burn this when you have read and understand what you have to do"

Muna gave the letter to Darius, she held her finger to her lips. He took it, read it, and read it again.

"Do you think that this is genuine, has our son found a way to get us away from here?" he whispered.

"Don't you think anything is better than our present situation? I don't care anymore; I can't live like this any longer. If there is a chance to see our son again, let's do it." Darius said nothing. He looked at the letter again and read it yet again, before whispering:

"You're right for all our sakes let us get it done." He gave the letter back to Muna, who took a box of matches from one of the cupboards, and after placing the thin sheet of paper and envelope in the sink, set fire to them. She waited until they had burnt through completely before washing the ashes away.

They went back into the living room, and for the sake of the listening device engaged in small talk. The conversation related about the shopping they had done, Darius mentioning the bargain he had got with the mangoes. He thought that the Guardian eavesdroppers would soon get bored of listening to the old couple's drivel. Muna mentioned that they would have to go back to the market in the morning, she wanted some tomatoes and there were some items of clothing she wanted to look at. They spent the rest of the day at home. After an evening meal. They decided to have an early night. It was going to be a long day tomorrow.

CHAPTER 23

Pegg was woken up by the sound of the burner phone, he had left it on the dressing table. He looked at his watch, it was eight o'clock. Beside him Pat stirred,

"Who is that at this time of the morning?" she murmured sleepily.

Pegg got out of bed and walked over to the dressing table.

"Hello".

"Archie, it's your visitor from last night, I'll keep it brief. As a result of speaking with the people in Norwich, the operation to get his guests to him will start today. I have told the host that if he gets the phone call he is expecting about the storage facility to carry on as normal. We have got this, but I will still need your help, but do not get your colleagues involved at all. Lives are at risk. And with respect we do not want them to throw obstructions in our way. I'll be in touch." The call finished before Pegg had a chance to reply.

"That was Chaim. Apparently the plan to get Mo's mum and dad out of Iran is in motion. He has told Mo if he gets a phone call regarding his storage facility on the Rash's Green industrial estate, he's is to act as if nothing has happened."

Pat sat up in bed, like Pegg she had nothing on. She got out of bed and put her dressing gown on, Pegg did likewise.

"Who does Chaim work for, apart from being a visiting lecturer?" she asked.

"I've worked that out. He's an Israeli spook. He could be working for Mossad their secret intelligence service, or Aman the military intelligence, or even Shin Bet the security service."

"Why would they be so involved?"

"It makes you think. Come on I need to let Fred out, and then I'll get us some breakfast."

Pegg went down to the kitchen to be met by a whimpering Fred, prancing at the back door. Pegg opened the door and the dog raced into the garden. Pegg shut the door again and started to lay the table for breakfast. Pat joined him shortly after. She had exchanged her dressing gown for jogging bottoms and a sweatshirt. Pegg prepared a breakfast of cereals, toast, boiled egg and a cafetiere of coffee. They ate and after clearing up, they got dressed. A short walk around the Green followed, and after collecting the Eastern Daily Press from the village shop, they returned home. Once in they sat down and read the paper. Pegg said:

"I don't know about you Pat, but I'm just wondering why the Israelis are taking such an interest in this whole matter. I mean they are investing a lot of effort and probably resources in getting a pair of elderly Iranians to safety."   "I am puzzled as well. I think the answer probably lies in the identity of the four Lebanese who were on the dashcam footage. Perhaps they were involved in some atrocity involving Israeli citizens or assets. The Israeli authorities have long memories, and they will not let things be. They will eventually take retribution, no matter how long they have to wait," she replied.

"You are right there. My concern is my commitment to Mo, and his mum and dad. That's why I'm involved. If I go to my people about this. Chaim's guvnors will be really pissed off, and so any goodwill we have with them will go down the tubes, and even at this stage I'm in too deep. No way will I have a job if I get my people involved."

"Well Archie you must do what you feel is right. If it helps I know where I stand with this."

"Where's that then?"

"You, and for that matter me, have decided on a course of action to help Mo out of his dilemma. So I feel that we should use any resources we have available to sort this thing out. We can't use official channels because we have broken too many rules. It's not so much a problem for me. It's an entirely different matter for a serving police officer. So in a way I'm in a better position to work on some aspects of the stuff we're doing for Mo. Let's see this through to the end."

"Well I'm glad that we have sorted that out. Now I've got to be back at work on Monday afternoon, so what shall we do over the weekend?"

As if to answer his question, the house phone rang: "Hi Archie, would you like to come over on Sunday?" said Angie.

"Of course," said Pegg looking at Pat, who was nodding her head, "what time do you want us to be there?"   "Oh any time after midday, we'll eat our lunch at about half one."

"We'll be there." Pegg continued to speak to her for the next five minutes. Pat indicated she would like to speak to her. After saying goodbye, he handed the phone over to Pat. The two women continued talking for the next ten minutes. Meanwhile Pegg made out a list of items he needed in Dereham. When Pat had finished on the phone, Pegg said:

"I need to get some stuff in for the next few days, so we'll take a trip into town, and maybe have some lunch, and after we'll go for a walk. How's that grab you?"

"I'm up for that Archie."

Thirty minutes later they were walking out of the Cherry Tree car park. Pat had taken her car as she wanted to fill up with fuel. Fred was left in the back of the X-trail. They visited a number of shops, buying groceries, items from the chemists, before returning to the car, where they put their shopping away and collected Fred. They made their way to the Bull in the High Street, where they had some lunch. They returned to Pat's X-Trail, and as there was nothing that would spoil amongst the groceries. They decided to go out to Foxley Woods, where there were some good walks. Prior to that Pat fuelled up the X-Trail.

It was gone five o'clock by the time they got back to Gressenhall. There were no messages on the answering machine. Pegg had checked his e-mails on his iPhone, there was nothing relevant there either.

They spent the rest of the evening talking and watching TV. At half past ten they were in bed. They slept well.

CHAPTER 24

In Iran, the Guardian whose responsibility it was to watch Darius and Muna Shaqaz was stood down from his task. His supervisor informed him he was needed for another job. The Shaqaz couple are so predictable, it was deemed that an absence of surveillance for a few days would not matter. The Guardian eavesdropper responsible for monitoring the elderly couple, had reported what they would be doing that day, from what he had heard of their conversations in the flat.

Darius and Muna had found it difficult to sleep, as a consequence they were quite tired when they got up. They stuck to their normal routine, going out at the usual time to the market. They just had their shopping bags with them, in which was their essential medication, and of course their passports. These documents had not been cancelled, something they could not comprehend. What they did not know was that their usefulness to Pejman would soon be at an end and what he had planned for them, the need for the documents would be over for ever. They went to the market, where they bought some tomatoes. After which they entered the small emporium at the side of the market. The clothes shop was open and Muna browsed for a little bit, she then joined Darius and they made their way through the back of the shop, and out of the back door, which led out into the small narrow street.

They saw a grey Toyota Hiace van parked on the other side of the street. They crossed the road and walked towards the vehicle and approached the grey van's right side. When they got there, the side door of the van slid open. A young woman dressed in black and wearing a Hijab exited the vehicle, and after taking their bags, helped them in one after the other into the back of the vehicle. Inside there were two seats contained within what looked like a false compartment. The seats were recliners and were surprisingly comfortable. She made Muna and Darius comfortable, after which she closed the van door and sat on a small bench next to Muna. She tapped the bulkhead on the front right side and the vehicle drove off. The van continued on its journey for about thirty minutes before it stopped.

The side door was opened, and the young woman was joined by another woman and a man. The other woman was dressed identically as the first woman, whilst the man was dressed in a woollen coat and hat, similar to many country people in that part of west Asia. The man spoke first in Farsi before continuing in English, he said:

"We are going to get you to safety. We will get you over the border into Pakistan, it is about a hundred miles away.. The roads are quite good, so we will be there in about three hours. Once we are in Pakistan you will be taken to a safe house, where you will rest. We have been given funds for you to purchase, such essentials, as toiletries, clothing, and of course suitcases. When you have rested, some other people will take you to Karachi, where you catch a flight to Qatar, and then on to Amsterdam Schiphol. You will be met there by your son. There are some primitive facilities here if you wish to use them. I advise you to do so, as we will not be stopping for the next three hours."

The van had stopped in a wooded area, there was a cinder brick block with a corrugated iron roof. They were toilets, with signs in Farsi saying "Men" at one end and "Women" at the other. After using the toilets the party boarded the van again. This time prior to moving off, the compartment door was closed, and crates of fruit were piled in covering the compartment. Within the part of the van in which they were sitting, Darius and Muna were warm and comfortable, in spite of the cold, damp weather outside. They were apprehensive, but at the same time, very excited at the prospect of seeing their son again. The young woman stayed with them within the compartment. She would not say who she or her colleagues were. Whilst she spoke fluent Persian, the conversation was conducted mainly in English.

"Who are you people, who risk your lives to rescue an old couple like us," asked Muna?

"It's best you don't know anything about us or our motives, but there are many of us working like this in the unhappy country that is our Iran. God willing there will be a day when our services will no longer be required. That's all I can tell you. Please do not ask any more about who we are. Now onto other matters. If we stop at all, please remain silent and leave it to my colleagues to deal with anything until we get to the safe house. I suggest you try and get some sleep."

It was good advice, Darius and Muna were very tired after having had a bad night. They were soon asleep. The journey was uneventful, and they reached Pakistan. Their passage through border post was eased with the gift of fruit to the policeman who, after a cursory glance at their

132

documents and a brief rummage through the back of the van, waved them through.

Forty minutes later the van stopped again. This time the vehicle had pulled into a walled compound within a small town in the province of Baluchistan. The main house was a fairly modest affair. The side door of the van was opened and the crates covering the compartment were unloaded, next the three people within the compartment got out. Darius and Muna were ushered into the house. The woman who had travelled with them in the back of the van, who they only knew as Maryam, stayed with them, whilst the van drove out of the compound. They never saw the van or the other two people who were with it again. There were two people in the house. They appeared to be local to the area. Maryam spoke to them in a language which neither Muna nor Darius understood. It was not Urdu, a tongue which they had some knowledge of. Maybe it was a local Baluchi dialect.

"We need to go out and do a little shopping," Maryam said to them. "One of these people will take you to a local emporium, where you'll be able to get everything you need. In the meantime I need your passports, to get a visa for the
United Kingdom. Don't ask me how, but it will be done for you in time for your flight from Karachi."

Muna and Darius accompanied the woman from the house to the local emporium, where they purchased a couple of suitcases, toiletries, underwear, nightwear, some tops, and trousers. All the items were paid for in Pakistani rupees. After an hour they returned to the house. Maryam had not yet returned. They ate a meal, after which they were shown to a bedroom. Their purchases had been taken to the room prior to their meal. They were tired, and both lay on their beds, and soon they were asleep.

The following morning, they were roused early, and by seven o' clock they were on the road, to Karachi. Maryam had returned their passports which had been endorsed with visitors' visas for the United Kingdom. She also had tickets for their flight to Amsterdam's Schiphol airport. At midday they arrived at Jinnah International Airport, which was located to the east of the city. An hour later they were on their way to Amsterdam's Schiphol airport, via Qatar.

CHAPTER 25

Mashrani did not drive to Southwold, instead he went directly to the industrial estate at Reydon. He parked outside the main roller door of the unit and went to the side door and rang the bell. After a short wait, the door was opened by Naji Azzi who locked the door again after Mashrani entered. He went into the office where he could see there was a camp bed and a sleeping bag on it. There was some of the detritus of half eaten food and takeaway cartons. Mashrani said:

"Why do you have to live like animals, tidy this shit up now. I need to brief you all. Do it now."

Azzi looked at Mashrani in a sullen manner before he went about clearing up the office Mashrani was now in a foul mood. He called the others using Azzi's phone. "Yusef," said Mashrani, "I want you here at the unit, now."

"All of us, up there?"

"In the name of the Prophet, why does everyone have to be told twice. Yes, do it now!" shouted Mashrani and ended the call.

Whilst they waited for the others to arrive, Mashrani asked if there had been any issues with other people from units on the estate. Azzi had said that nobody seemed to be interested in the unit and what was in it. Mashrani checked the DAF van. The contents in the back had not been disturbed, he was pleased that his instructions regarding the van's load had been complied with. Azzi continued to tidy up, putting the rubbish in a bin bag. The sound of a vehicle pulling up outside caused Mashrani to look out of the unit's office window. It was the green Ford van. Yusef and the other two got out, Azzi let them in, and after dumping the bin bag in the rubbish skip came back into the unit, locking the office door behind him. Mashrani had laid out the OS map of the North Wendlesham area, as well as his laptop, and the notes and sketches he had made. He spoke to them in Arabic:

"Right brothers, at last I am able to share with you our new plan, which has had the approval of our superiors in Iran."

He went on to explain about the area where they would be operating. He discussed who would be doing what and where. He showed them Google Earth images of the airfield, and also the photographs he had taken from the viewing area. He had uploaded the images from his phone onto the laptop. After he had explained what their mission would be, he talked on more personal matters.

"Brothers when I came here today, I found that the state of these premises were like that of a dirty byre. A farmer would not permit his animals to live in such filth. I am informed that you are the best warriors that could be found. The Prophet, peace be upon him, taught the importance of cleanliness. I expect the same of my soldiers. So if you wish to continue to serve our cause you need to sort yourselves out. Yusef you will make sure that my wishes are adhered to."

Yusef, looked gravely and nodded. Mashrani continued:

"When we leave both this unit, and the static, I want it to look as if we have never been here. All rubbish and any other waste must be removed, placed in the appropriate receptacles, and anything which may be linked to us either destroyed or taken with us. Now I will be leaving you I will not be coming back here. I will phone you when I want you to join me. I will give you three-hours' notice when I want you to leave here, this will give you a chance to pack, and clean up.'

'One other thing Yusef. I want you to test the electronic modifications to the stuff we'll be using on our mission. There will not be another opportunity, do this when I go.

"It will be done", Yusef replied.

"Good, I'll take my leave now. God be with you brothers." He gave them some briefing notes he had previously written down, after which he left and drove back to Norwich and onto the hotel near the Norfolk Showground.

* * *

At the same time as Mashrani had got to his room in the hotel, in another part of city, the KLM flight from Schiphol arrived at Norwich International Airport. The Shaqaz family in its entirety cleared customs and went to the passenger exit. Mo walked through with his arm around Muna, whilst Darius pushed a trolley with their luggage. There to meet them was Esi. After a brief introduction, Muna embraced him and kissed him on both cheeks, her eyes were full of tears, she had not really stopped crying since she was met at Schiphol by Mo. Esi shook hands with Darius, who, on letting go of the trolley, embraced him.

"Bless you my son, you have healed our Mohammed's heartbreak. Now we have two sons!"

"Come on let's get you all home. You must be so exhausted after your epic journey," Esi said, ushering all out of building and onto the car park to the car. After they were all loaded up. Esi drove back to the house in Costessey.

Once they were inside the house. They went up to the bedroom which had been prepared for Muna and Darius. Mo and Esi left them to unpack. Mo made a call on the burner phone to Eban:

"I am pleased to tell you the mission has been accomplished. I can never repay you for what you have done," he said.

"I am very pleased for you. You will be repaying us by acting as if the mission never took place. Keep them safe and out of the public eye for now. We do not think that you are under observation at this time, but just as a precaution keep everything under wraps. Let me know as soon as you get the phone call, I will let Archie know as well. Stay safe my friend, may the Lord be with you."

Mo and Esi were joined by Muna and Darius, who had unpacked and were well on the way to settling in. Mo explained that they needed to remain in the house for a few days. They were quite happy with this, after all they had endured enough excitement over the past 48 hours. It was time to wind down. After dinner, they spent the rest of the evening talking about the future. Darius and Muna were hoping to be able to re-start work as teachers. They were fluent English speakers and possessed skills in subjects which were much needed by the education authorities. Muna was a Mathematics teacher, Darius had taught Science and Electrical Engineering. At the moment they only had permission to stay in the United Kingdom for six months. That would have to change if they wanted to engage in work, and ultimately settle on a permanent basis. It had been a long day, and everyone went to bed happy and content. They slept very well. For Muna and Darius it was the best night's sleep they had had in a long time.

CHAPTER 26

Mashrani was up quite early on this Sunday morning. He had booked a small holiday cottage in Stanfield. It slept six, and due to the time of year, the rates were very reasonable. It was in a fairly remote location and was hidden from the road outside by a thick row of leylandii cypress trees. Mashrani thought that it gave the impression of intense gloom and ugliness; it was probably why it was available. He couldn't see many people spending their time in such depressing surroundings. However on the plus side there was ample parking in front and to the side of the house, and the location was about five miles north of Dereham, and four miles south of North Wendlesham airfield. He would move all his assets there just prior to the operation, meanwhile, it was time to make the call to Mohammed Shaqaz. After a slight delay Mo, who was at home, it being Sunday, picked up:

"Mr Shaqaz," Mashrani spoke in Farsi, "It's time for you to help your country."

"Yes," replied Mo sounding really nervous and frightened, "how are mama and papa. Are they well and safe?"

"Of course and they will remain so as long as you do precisely what I say. This evening I want you at your storage unit, make sure there is enough room to park a seven tonne box van inside. Can you do that for me?"

"There is a delivery coming on Monday morning, I do not know if there will be room."

"I'm not going to argue Shaqaz, just make sure I can park my van inside. You know what will happen if you don't." Playing the part well, Mo interrupted:

"Please, please don't hurt them, I will do whatever you want. The unit will be ready." he wailed.

"Calm yourself, you do as you're told, and everything will be fine, now this is what I want you to do."

Mashrani talked for another for another five minutes, after which he said:

"I don't have to tell you that this call stays between us. You don't tell anyone about it. You understand Shaqaz?"

"Yes! Yes, I'll tell nobody." With that Mashrani ended the call.

Mo leaned back in the armchair in the sitting room where he had taken the call and smiled to himself. I hope that my act went down well, he thought. He had not been expecting the call so soon. He had left his parents sleeping, whilst he and Esi had breakfast. Esi was duty solicitor today, ready to take calls from either the Wymondham or the Great Yarmouth Police Investigation Centres. So far this morning his services were not required.

Mo took out the burner phone and called Eban:

"Mashrani has told me that my company's storage facility is required this evening."

"What time?"

"Mashrani wasn't specific, but it was to be available from six onwards. He wants to park a seven-tonne box van inside."

"Is it large enough for that?"

"It will be, but I need to do a bit of re-organising. I've got a delivery on Monday, which I may have to divert to my main shop. It will be tight, but with a bit of tweaking, I should be able to get the stuff into the stock room at the main store. Chaim, I forgot to tell you, I have CCTV in the unit."

"That's brilliant. This puts a different light on things."
"Our insurers recommended that we do this, as it would reduce our premiums. In addition to obviously recording any break-ins, it does prevent some in-house theft. Not that my employees would do that, but we do get all sorts coming to the warehouse, delivery drivers, maintenance workers, that sort of thing."

"Briefly explain how the system works."

"There are four cameras, one covers the office reception area, there are two more covering the inside of the warehouse, and there is one covering the outside. The live feed goes into a unit which is located behind a vent. The whole system can be accessed from either my office from an app on my desktop or my iPhone"

"Does Mashrani know about this?"

"No he has never asked me about anything like this. The only thing he may want to know about, is the burglar alarm. He may or not wish to use it. Any way I'll give him the code to disarm it."

"Good, don't let him know about the CCTV system unless he asks. Are the cameras obvious?"

"No they are not. Unless you know what you're looking for, you'll not find them."

"Great, this gives us a tremendous advantage. Call me again when the van arrives."

Mo ended the call and then rang Pegg. He gave him a resume of the conversation he had just had with Eban.

"So we'll be able to have a ring side seat of all the activity going on in the warehouse. It gets better and better," said Pegg.

They talked for a further five minutes, before Pegg continued:

"Look Mo I shall be away from the house for the rest of the day, we'll be back home at about five. If you need to speak before then, call me on my mobile."

*　*　*

After finishing the phone call to Mo, Mashrani called Yusef Haddad.

"Yusef, it is time to move out. You and the others clear out the static caravan and make your way up to the unit at Reydon. I will meet you there in a couple of hours or so. Make sure the static is clean and tidy. I don't want any complaints coming back to me about the state of the place. I will brief you further when I meet you. Have checked out the kit?"

"It is all working."

"God be praised! I'll be with you soon."

When he had finished speaking to Yusef, Mashrani collected the rest of his stuff and loaded the items into the VW, and after leaving his room key at reception, he drove to the nearby superstore where he purchased food for a couple of days for the five of them. After this he drove onto the eastbound lane of the A47. Two hours later he arrived at the industrial unit in Reydon. The Ford van was parked outside. It being a Sunday, the estate was empty, and the rest of the units were closed. He entered the unit to find Yusef and the three others inside. The unit had been swept clean, and apart from items of outer clothing; nothing had been left lying around.

"Right, brothers", said Mashrani, once they were all gathered in the office of the unit, "we shall not be returning here. We are coming to the end of our stay in this country, and we will soon be completing our mission.'

'We will be going to the last location we'll be staying at. When we get there, I want you to get your stuff into the house before we go to the place where we will be keeping the van. You will be pleased to hear that it will not be necessary for anyone to remain with the van. We have been able to "persuade" the owner to lend us the facility where we will be keeping the van. He knows what will happen to his family if he dares to do anything to interfere with our equipment or the mission."

'So you Yusef and Ahmad will take the DAF van, Kaled and Naji the Ford van. Any questions?" They said nothing. 'I will lead, the DAF comes behind me, and the Ford takes up the rear. Let's get going."

They left the unit and Mashrani secured it. He got into the VW and waited whilst the rest got into the other two vehicles. Once the other vehicles had started up, he drove out of the estate followed by the DAF and Ford vans. Mashrani drove northwards towards Lowestoft, and then onto Norwich, where the vehicles headed west along the A47. Mashrani led the small convoy through Dereham and north out of the town to Beetley and then onto the B1145, where they turned off into Stanfield, five minutes later they pulled into the driveway of the holiday cottage. The journey had taken them about two and a half hours. It was still four hours before Mashrani was due to meet up with Mo at the warehouse. He unlocked the cottage and showed them in. There were three bedrooms, one of which had a double bed, whilst the other two each had two single beds. Mashrani gave himself the room with the double bed, the rest were allocated the other two rooms. The food from the VW was brought in and a meal was prepared and eaten.

* * *

Pegg received Mo's call on the burner phone which Chaim had given to him. He had the phone on speaker when he took the call from Mo.

"Right Pat we must make sure that we are back from Angie's by six o'clock at the latest."

"That's fine with me. Is there any way that Mo could get the feed from the CCTV to us somehow?"

"Well I had not thought of that. It would be good if we could. I'll ask Angie about how we could go about it." said Pegg.

Later they made their way to Swaffham, where they spent the rest of the day with the Masons, Angie, Ross and the baby. They dined on a delicious roast, followed by apple pie. After the meal they went to the park. Catherine Rose played on the swings, and Fred played with his tatty and heavily soiled tennis ball, running after the thrown sphere, and retrieving it again and again. Angie had told Pegg and Pat, if they got the access codes from Mo, they should be able to log into Mo's warehouse CCTV system from any iPhone, tablet or PC providing the relevant app was downloaded.

Pegg and Pat left the Masons at half past five and made their way back to Gressenhall. Eban was waiting in his car, which he had parked outside the Reading Room. When he saw Pegg's Land Rover draw into the drive of Pegg's house, he got out of the car and walked over. He met Pegg as he was getting out of the vehicle.

"Chaim, when did you get here?"

"I've been here about for about half an hour, I wanted a talk with you both, before I go over to Dereham, where we shall be discreetly observing what happens."

Pegg led them into the house. Eban declined any refreshments. They went into the living room. Eban began by telling them what had happened during the day. He said that he had been to Mo's house where he had a long talk with Mo, Esi, and Mo's parents.

"It is my belief, and this is shared by others, whose identities I'm not in a position to reveal, that the persons who are threatening Mo's family are terrorists. They are in the process of planning some outrage. It would appear after

Mashrani's escapade at Marham airfield, the type of target he is after attacking is military rather than civilian.'" Eban paused before continuing, "I'll level with you; we are after taking out Mashrani and the other four."

"By taking out do you mean killing them?" interrupted Pegg.

"I hope it won't come to that; we would rather render them into some sort of custody. They will have a great deal of information to give up, especially Mashrani."

"What do you mean by 'render'? asked Pegg.

"Archie, my people have put a lot of resources into resolving this situation. We have snatched Mo's parents out of the clutches of the IRGC. We have a real chance of

144

destroying the Quds Force presence in this part of the British Isles, and maybe beyond. But in order to achieve this we must do it my way. If you are having second thoughts about this, then now is the time to tell me. I will have to carry on with just Mo."

"Chaim neither of us wants to back out now, but in view of my position as a serving police officer, I feel that maybe we should be informing the appropriate authorities about this and what we know."

"I have the greatest respect for the British Judicial system, but once this becomes an official investigation, our people will have no say in it. We will no longer be able to act on our own initiative and in the end we'll lose any right to interview Mashrani and the rest of them, and in addition we would lose valuable intelligence. You must remember the four Lebanese Hezbollah have committed serious crimes, including murder, for which they are still unpunished. I'm sure Mashrani is not innocent either. Can you see them being put on trial here when the crimes they committed were outside British jurisdiction?"   "So what are we to do?" asked Pat.

"I hope that you are going to help me to stop whatever outrage this motley crew are planning. We start this evening by finding out what they are planning to do in Mo's warehouse. Now are you with me on this or not." "We're in" said Pat, looking at Pegg.

"We're in," repeated Pegg, thinking to himself, 'what the heck have I let myself into.'   Eban looked at his watch.

"Right it's time to get going. Where is the best place to park our cars?"

"We'll go in my Land Rover; you follow us Chaim."

They left Gressenhall and drove into Dereham and twenty minutes later, they had parked up at the south end of Bertie Ward Way, behind a large pantechnicon. Pat and Pegg went and sat with Eban in his car. Eban moved his car slightly forward, the new position gave them a good line of sight to Mo's warehouse, but at the same time they were hidden from anyone looking in the opposite direction. It was nearly dark, but the streetlighting offered adequate illumination to the area in front of the units. They were about 100 yards from the front of the warehouse.

CHAPTER 27

Mo arrived at the warehouse some minutes before the time Mashrani had told him to be there. He parked his car immediately outside the office door, got out and unlocked the office door. Once inside he walked over to the bleeping alarm box and disarmed the alarm system. His burner phone vibrated in his trouser pocket:

"Mo we are about 100 metres away. We can see the front of the unit. We'll stay put until after Mashrani and co have left. Act as we discussed Mashrani must go way with the impression that you are terrified with what will happen to your mum and dad if Mashrani thinks that you will doublecross him. The Lord be with you," with that Eban ended the call.

Mo returned the burner phone back to the same pocket. He went into the nearly empty warehouse, and unbolted the bottom of the roller door, after which he returned to the office. He did not have to wait too long before Mashrani's small convoy arrived. Mo went to the door of the office as the three vehicles pulled up. Mashrani got out of the VW and directed the DAF to reverse up to the roller door. Speaking Farsi, Mashrani said:

"Get the door open, now."

Mo went back inside the unit and pressed the button at the side of the roller door. The door started to open. Once it was high enough, Mashrani guided the DAF as it reversed all the way into the warehouse.

"Right get it closed again."

Mo operated the other button which closed the door. Once it was closed he bolted the bottom of the door.

146

"Now you said this place is alarmed," Mashrani said.

"Yes it is. If it goes off I get a message on my phone. I can then get someone to come and check it out. Sometimes I do it, or a member of my staff does it. To tell the truth since I have rented the warehouse, it has never been broken into, and neither have we had an alarm activation, false or otherwise. I suppose you want the code to arm and disarm the alarm?" asked Mo.

"No Shaqaz, and I'll tell you why. You are going to make sure that this place is not disturbed in any way whatsoever. You will secure this place after we have gone, and when we want it opened up, you will do it immediately I do not care what you are doing at the time, you understand Shaqaz?"

"Yes of course."

"I'm glad about that Shaqaz, because you know what will happen if I have any cause to believe you're not complying with my wishes. I will arrange for your father to be permanently eliminated, and if you still continue to disobey me, the same will happen to your mother. You understand me, you stinking little queer?"

Mo baulked at this slight, it was very difficult to contain his rage. He played the part, and whimpered,

"Please sir, do not hurt mama and papa. I have done everything you want; they will still be okay, won't they?"

"Of course they will be fine. Do as we ask, and all will be well," said Mashrani, knowing full well that Pejman will have them murdered along with Mo, once the mission was over. Mashrani continued.

"Now is that your car parked next to ours?"

"Yes."

"Good, we will be in here for about twenty minutes, leave us now and wait in your car. One of us will come and tell you when we are ready to leave. Now go!"

Mo went outside and Mashrani shut the office door behind him, locking it. When Mo had left Mashrani gave instructions to Yusef-al-Haddad. Haddad and the three others started to take items from the back of the van. Meanwhile Mashrani got his satellite phone and spoke to Pejman in Iran.

"Well what have you got to tell me, something good I hope, after the last debacle," sneered Pejman.

"Sir I'm happy to say that we are in position where we'll be able to carry out the mission very shortly."

"How shortly?"

"Within the next three or so days."

"That's good, and is our little queer co-operating?"
"Yes he's petrified that we will hurt his parents if he does not do as we want. I told him his father gets it first, and if he

fucks with us again, mama gets it as well"

"Good we'll kill all of them once your mission is completed. The parents will be done here. You will eliminate Shaqaz."

"Understood sir."

"Right get to it. The next call I get from you will be to inform me of the success of the mission." Pejman ended the call.

"Yusef are you guys finished," asked Mashrani, switching to Arabic.

"Boss we are about done. What will we do about Shaqaz?

"He helps us for now, once we're finished he will be eliminated by us. Our brothers in Iran will do the same to his parents. For now keep this to yourself, the others do not need to know. Now tell Ahmad to bring Shaqaz back in"

* * *

Mo went out and got into his car and waited. He was seething with rage. It wasn't long before the burner phone vibrated in his pocket.

148

"Mo what's happening?"

Mo crouched down in his car so that anyone looking out of the office window could not see him. Although with it being dark, it would be difficult to see into a parked car, even with the benefit of the ambient illumination from the street lighting.

"They told me to wait outside, I suppose they are unloading stuff from the van, and they don't want me to see what it is. Still when I access the CCTV, we'll be able to see what it is they are doing"

"Have they cottoned onto the CCTV system."

"No, they don't seem to be aware of any cameras inside the warehouse. Mashrani is a vile bastard, he's threatening to kill mama and papa, if I fail to do what he wants. He's insulted me personally; I was hard put not to give him a good hiding. I'm so angry Chaim, I nearly lost it. But at least mama and papa are in a safe place now. None of those filthy swine can hurt them"

"Just hang on in there Mo, everything will turn out fine, trust me. We got mum and dad back to you and we'll get this thing sorted, but you are key to our success. Okay I'll leave you to it, we'll keep watching you, and we'll join you when they have left."

Mo put the burner back in his pocket, He switched on the car radio and listened to some music. Eventually one of the Lebanese came out. He walked to the car and opened the driver's door.

"You come!" the man said in heavily accented English. Mo followed him into the office. He was joined by Mashrani and the other three Lebanese, they were all carrying sports equipment bags. The bags appeared to be heavy. The three men went out and loaded the bags into the Ford van, two of them got into the van, one into the driver's seat and the other into the passenger seat. The third waited at the door.

"We are leaving now Shaqaz," said Mashrani again speaking Farsi, "remember what I have told you, the lives of your parents are in your hands."

Mashrani and the rest of them left the warehouse, leaving Mo to secure the building.

* * *

"Right Archie," said Eban, "it looks like they are on the move. What I would like to do is for you to follow them and see where they are going. I suspect that they have got some really naughty stuff in those bags. Don't let them suspect that you are tailing them. Oh before you go take these"

Eban reached into the glove compartment and retrieved a pair of disc-shaped objects which were four centimetres in diameter and a centimetre thick.

"Archie these are transponders, if you can, I'd like you to put one under each of the two vehicles. They will enable us to track them and locate them at any time of the day. You see the tab at the top? You pull it off, and just fix it underneath, press it on, there is a form of epoxy resin, which goes off almost immediately it is exposed to air. The device is impossible to move without cutting away the surrounding material of the place to which the transponder is attached." He gave the devices to Pegg.

"No worries Chaim. Where shall we meet up again?"
"Pat and I will join Mo, and maybe we'll get an idea of what sort of stuff they've been carrying in that van. When you have finished go back to your house, and we'll see you there."

"Okay see you soon," said Pegg he got out of the car and went over to the Land Rover.

Fred was sitting on the driver's seat, Pegg tickled his ear before pushing him over onto the passenger seat. He waited for Mashrani and his men to leave the warehouse. Ten minutes later he saw three men coming out of the warehouse; each was carrying a large sports bag, similar to those which cricketers use for their kit. The men walked to the back of the Ford van and placed their bags in the back of the vehicle, after which, two of them got into the van, whilst the third waited by the door. A short while later another man emerged, and he was joined by two others. All three then got into the Polo.

The Polo drove away from the warehouse, followed by the Ford van. Pegg started up the Land Rover and went after them. He waited at the junction of Rashes Green and Bertie Ward Way, until the taillights of the end vehicle disappeared around the curve, before he pulled out and followed them. He continued to the end of Rashes Green and turned right onto South Green, driving toward the town centre. The other two vehicles had approached the traffic lights with London Road. The lights turned to green, and they turned left. Pegg guessed they would be going north through town. He kept his distance and drove down the High Street. He surmised that they would be going through Market Place and onto Quebec Road.

He was right; still keeping his distance, he followed the two vehicles past the golf club. They turned left off Holt Road and into Beetley. Fortunately for Pegg there were two cars between his vehicle and the Ford van. This state of affairs lasted until these two cars turned right onto the B1145 at East Bilney whilst Mashrani's two cars turned left, and after a short distance turned right off the B1145 and onto Back Lane, Stanfield. Pegg turned the Land Rover's lights off when the two cars ahead turned into Back Lane. Back Lane was very narrow, and as a consequence the vehicles travelled slowly.

As Pegg approached the turning he could see the taillights of the van about 100 metres ahead. Pegg had the advantage of knowing every part of this area of Norfolk, so he felt quite safe about proceeding without any form of illumination. They drove past Stanfield church and continued for about another half a mile before the brake lights of both vehicles came on. The lead vehicle turned off the lane, followed by the Ford van. Pegg guessed where they had gone. He pulled up onto a beet pad and exited the vehicle. He left Fred, and walked up to where the two vehicles had pulled in.

He got to the point where Mashrani's little convoy had turned off the road. The row of leylandii conifers to his right masked the house from the road. He looked into the driveway between the conifers. There was no outside lighting, but the lights from the house shone out, and illuminated the parking area to the front for about three or four metres. The two cars which were parked in front of the house were mostly in the shadows.

He kept to the shadowy area and made his way to the Polo, where he attached the first of Eban's transponders behind the rear offside wheel arch. Prior to attaching it he rubbed off some of the accumulated dust and mud from the inside of the wheel arch. After he had finished attaching it, he rubbed some of the mud over the device. He pulled at the transponder, it did not move, it was solidly glued in position. Next he moved over to the Ford van and repeated the process. When he'd finished attaching the devices. He moved back into the shadows. The curtains in the downstairs rooms of the house were not drawn. Pegg decided to wait before he left. He was curious as to the contents of the sports bags, which Mashrani's henchmen had been carrying. Keeping in the shadows he made his way to the right of the house and stopped when he was next to what appeared to be the living room. He eased forward and looked into the room. It was the living room. It was quite small, there were two armchairs and a small sofa, a coffee table separated the armchairs and the sofa, which backed up to the window. Mashrani was sitting on the sofa next to him was one of the Lebanese, spread on the table was a map. The two men had their backs to Pegg. There was no sign of the sports bags. Pegg decided to move around to the back of the building. Again he moved round with his back to the wall, feeling with his hands and his feet for any obstruction. He was glad that he did, as he came across a water butt at the rear corner of the house, around which was stacked some timber and roof tiles; these could have been knocked down had he not been exercising care, the resulting crash would have alerted the occupants of the house. As he got to the butt, he could see the lights from what must have been the kitchen, shining out onto the space at the back of the house.

Pegg crept past the butt and around the rear corner of the building, he got himself into a position where he could look through the window without being seen himself. He was right, it was the kitchen, and what he saw appalled and frightened him.

CHAPTER 28

Eban and Pat joined Mo at the warehouse. Eban had with him a messenger bag. They went into the main part of the building and to where the DAF van was parked. The van was locked both the doors to the cab and the shutter at the rear of the vehicle had been secured by Mashrani and his crew had left.

"Before we start, I suggest I interrogate the CCTV, and maybe we can see what these bastards were up to when they chucked me out of the building," said Mo. "How are you going to do that?" asked Eban

"The wonders of the iPhone, I have an app!" Mo proceeded to tap into the device, and a few moments later, its screen showed four quartered images. He brought up one of the images to main screen. The other two were at each of Mo's elbows craning their necks to see the small screen.

"This one is the image from the camera showing the action within the main part o0f the warehouse I'll bring up playback".

"I think it would be a good idea if you erased any record of us being in here, just in case."

"It's done! Now it's showtime!"

Mo tapped the device again and the image showed Mo leaving. One of the four Lebanese opened the back of the box van. He climbs up into back of van and is joined by one of his colleagues. They drag two of the cardboard crates onto the loading platform. The platform is lowered, and the crates are dragged off onto the floor of the warehouse. The crates are opened, and items are taken out.

"What the devil are those asked Pat?"

"They look like rifles, and what are those other things is that a rocket and something else?"

Eban looked closer at the small screen and exclaimed: "Bloody hell! Those are M16 Armalite rifles, and the rocket as you call it Pat is in fact part of the SA7 Grail Strela -2 system. There is the rocket and its launcher.

"What would those be used for," asked Mo.

"Well it's a handheld anti-aircraft missile system. It's a Russian system, been around for quite a long time, the Soviet Union started equipping the Red Army with it in the 1970s. It's just as deadly in the right hands in today's military environment. It has been modified and improved since it was first introduced. The IDF air units have been fired on by these weapons. The Syrian army and Iraqi forces under Saddam were equipped with these systems. This is extremely worrying."

"Would they be using them against airliners or something like that?"

"From what we know so far it looks as if it's some form of attack on military aircraft."

"Well they have only taken two missiles and one launcher with them. It looks as if the rest of the stuff is on the back of the box van. We need to get a closer look."

"We don't want to get caught doing it, what if Mashrani and the rest of those bastards come back?" said Mo "Well hopefully we'll know if they are on the move back here if Archie has managed to fix the transponders to the Ford and the VW. Which reminds me I need to fix one the box van, before we do anything else," replied Eban. He retrieved another of the devices he had given to Pegg from his pocket, and fixed it under the box van, when he had done that he looked at the lock on the door to the back of the vehicle.

"Right before we start, Mo, is there any way we can find out what these people were saying before they left, I mean whilst you were waiting in your car?"

Mo got tapped his device again. He brought up the image of Masrani in the warehouse office. He was alone, speaking on his phone. He adjusted the volume.

"He's speaking Farsi, he says he's in a position to carry out the operation in there or so days. Then he says I am petrified as to what will happen to my parents. He then says understood sir. I am afraid I could not get what the person on the other end of the phone was saying. The call ends and one of the Lebanese comes into the office, and the conversation switches to Arabic I assume."

"May I", said Eban.

Mo paused the playback and handed the device to Eban.

"The Lebanese, who I believe is Yusef, says that they are ready. Then Yusef asks what they are going to do about

Mo."

Eban listened to the playback further, he paused the recording, and said nothing.

"Well what did he say?" asked Pat.

Eban paused for a while before saying:

"Mashrani told Yusef that Mo helps them for now, but when they have finished, he will be "eliminated" and the same goes for his parents in Iran."

Mo's face went grey, and he would have collapsed to the floor if Pat had not caught him. She guided him to a to a box and sat him down. Pat had her arms round his shoulders.

"Oh Mo, I'm so sorry, but we'll get through this, we are all here for you."

Mo gently squeezed her hand and rested his head on her chest. He sighed and said:

"These pieces of shit were lying to me all the time. I'm so pleased that Eban's people got mama and papa out from under these beasts' noses. If I had one of their guns I would eliminate the lot of them myself. I'll do whatever it takes to

stop Mashrani and his thugs."

"Well we're all with you there Mo," said Eban, before continuing, "right let's see if these things are working." He pulled a smart phone out of his pocket and tapped in a code.

"Yup it looks like Archie has planted the two devices I gave him, and the one I've just put on the van works as well." As he spoke one of his burner phones rang:

"Hello Archie, how are you getting on?"

"Bloody heck Eban do you know these arseholes have enough stuff to fight a small war?"

"It seems that they have unloaded four M16's, some boxes of ammunition and two handheld anti-aircraft missiles and a launcher," replied Eban.

"How do you know that?"

"We reviewed the CCTV, and there it was. Right Archie the transponders are working, so well done with that. Make your way back here. I don't think those guys will moving any more tonight. We'll know if they do. By the way, have you got any tools with you.?"

"I've got a toolbox in the back of my Land Rover."
"Great we may need it. Be as quick as you can." Eban finished the call and said to the other two:

156

"We need to get the back of the box van open. I don't think the lock is up to much."

He rummaged in his messenger bag and extracted a small tool roll, as well as some surgical gloves. He gave a pair to Mo and Pat and put a pair on as well.

"We don't want to be leaving our dabs all over the van," he said.

He took a pick from the roll and went back to the back of the van. After pulling the loading platform from its vertical to its horizontal position, he started to work on the lock, and a few moments later he was rolling the door to the back of the van upwards. He reached inside the back and the operated the mechanism which lowered the platform.

"Let's see what we have got, I don't think all of us should step on at once. Pat hop on, Mo if you would be ready for us to pass some of the lighter stuff down"

Pat and Eban were lifted up and went into the back of the van. There were four empty cardboard crates. Eban took a photo of the position of these and the rest of the already opened crates. The empty crates were then passed to Mo, who stacked them at the side of the vehicle. To describe the opened crates as such was a bit of a misnomer. The gaffer tape which had originally sealed the crates, had been cut along its length with what may have been a craft knife. They dragged two of the crates over to the loading platform and lowered them to the floor. Mo dragged them clear, the platform was raised, and two more crates were dragged onto it, and again lowered to the floor. The process was repeated until the back of the van was empty.

The crates were placed on the floor in the order which they had come off the van. They lifted the flaps on the top of the crates and looked inside at their contents. Five of the crates each contained a launcher, it weighed 4.71

kg, and it was 1.47 metres long. Another ten crates each contained a missile.

"We need to be careful of those. They are the missiles, they fit onto the launchers. They have a 1.15 kg explosive warhead, and there is a solid fuel propellant as well which could be quite volatile, if mishandled. Still if they were going to explode prematurely it would have happened by now.

Let's put our phones in the office for now as a precaution. These chaps are quite heavy; they weigh nearly 10 kilos. At least we know how many missiles they have. It's a total of twelve."

Another four crates each contained a light aluminium framed stand, with four spiked spigots taped to the bottom of each of the stands. The final crate contained boxes of ammunition, both 9 mm and 5.56 mm.

"These launchers seem to have some sort of box on them and a lever which is attached to the firing mechanism," said Eban.

Pat had a closer look, after examining the item she said:

"I know what these are, I've been dealing with this sort of thing since we met in Norwich last year."

"What with anti-aircraft missiles Pat?"

"Don't be daft Chaim! I've been working with the boxes. They are switching devices. They are used in hundreds of applications. Stuff like switching central heating on and off, or arming burglar alarms, house lights, washing machines, the list is endless. We have been developing stuff for mobile phones and other devices. We're currently working on something which is confidential at the moment."

"So, Pat, these boxes mean that the missiles could be launched remotely, instead of some guy holding the launcher to his shoulder? So you could use a phone or similar device to operate the trigger mechanism."

158

"Providing you have either a good signal on your phone, or Wi-Fi for your device, yes you can."

Eban thought for a bit. He was thinking of a plan. As he was pondering the next steps to take, they heard a vehicle pulling up outside. It was Pegg. Mo let him in, Eban checked his device. Mashrani's vehicles were still at the house in Stanfield. Pegg came in, put the toolbox he had been carrying down, and looked into the crates and their contents of the open crates.

"This is serious stuff Chaim; those bastards are equipped to do some major damage to somewhere. What can we do about it?"

Eban explained what had happened in the warehouse whilst Mo was waiting outside, and the plans to murder Mo and his parents, had they been in Iran. Pegg said nothing, he looked at Mo, and then at Eban and Pat, finally he said:

"So is there anything we can do?"

"I think there is", said Pat, "if I can disable the switching devise on the launchers, that will be a start."

"You can do that?" asked Eban.

"I know these chaps inside out; now Archie, your toolbox please."

Pegg carried he toolbox over and opened the lid. Pat rummaged through and extracted some small screwdrivers and pincers. She removed the first of the devices from its launcher. She worked on it for about five minutes, and put it together again, before refitting it back onto launcher. For the next half hour she repeated the operation until all the devices were fitted back on the rest of the launchers. "Right that's all those done, those switching devices are completely Kaput."

"Well done Pat, now let's get all the stuff back on the van again, in reverse order. Mashrani must never know we have been in here. You okay now Mo?" "Thanks to Pat I am a lot better."

Thirty minutes later the box van had been reloaded and secured, its loading platform in the same position as the Lebanese had left it. Mo locked up the warehouse. Pegg looked at the time it was three o'clock, he was due to start his dayshift at Dereham in four hours. Still it was time well spent, even if he was going to suffer some sleep deprivation.

Before they departed, Eban explained to them, he would keep monitoring Masrani's vehicle movements. Any change in the whereabouts of Mashrani and his party, and he would let them know. He said there may be one or two strangers appearing on the scene, ignore them, they are part of my people One will be constantly in the vicinity of Mo. There was already a person looking out for Mo's

parents near to the house in Norwich.

CHAPTER 29

In Iran, the Guardian carrying out the surveillance of Mo's parents was back at his post. There had been some public disorder in a town to the west of Tehran. There was a lot of discontent about the price of fuel. Guardians of all ranks had been sent to deal with the disturbances, some like the young Guardian were withdrawn from their duties. The disorder had subsided rather than having to be put down. His absence from his post had brought a bit more excitement to the young man's boring routine. After being away for a week, he was not looking forward to his mindnumbing task again.

The target couple had still not made an appearance. It was gone ten o'clock in the morning, they should have been out and about by now to do a bit of food shopping. He waited for half an hour before calling his supervisor. The supervisor checked with the eavesdropper, no there were no sounds coming from the flat. He was told by the supervisor to check with the informant in the couple's block of flats.

The informant was not able to help, like the young Guardian, the informant had been away, but in hospital. The last time she had seen the Shaqazes was six days ago, just before she had to go into hospital.

The Guardian decided to visit the flat. He knocked at the door and got no answer. What if they were dead? He banged hard again on the door, again there was no reaction.

He called his supervisor again. The supervisor arranged for some Guardians to assist the young man in gaining entry to the flat. He was joined by the others, and together they broke front door down. The flat was empty, but all the couple's meagre collection of belongings and clothing were still there. It did not appear that they had left to travel anywhere, as their things were still there. The Guardian was called back to his barracks. He was interviewed by his immediate superiors. In spite of his protestations that he had been away for the past seven days, he was deemed to have been responsible for failing to inform them of the couple's disappearance.

A search of the area was carried out, the market traders were asked if they had seen Mo's parents. If any of them knew anything about it, they were hardly going to share that knowledge with the people who they felt were one of the reasons for the country's poor economic state of affairs.

Their enquires drew a blank. Some of the Guardians started to think that maybe an overzealous member, had taken it upon themselves to carry out Pejman's orders prematurely. That theory started to gain credence, in spite of there being any evidence to say that this was the case.

When Pejman found out that the couple had disappeared. His rage knew no bounds. He had both the young Guardian and the informant arrested. In spite of being brutally interrogated both the informant and the young Guardian were unable to give Pejman the answers he wanted. In view of his recent conversation with Mashrani, and Mohammed Shaqaz's continued acquiescence he started to take the view that Mo's parents had indeed been murdered and their remains disposed of. He realised that he created such a climate of fear amongst his own underlings, that nobody was willing to admit to the killings.

The plans in England were too far advanced for him to start to bother Mashrani about the welfare of these useless old fools. The matter was now closed. All that had to happen was the elimination of their son, and that was in hand.

CHAPTER 30

The following day, Pegg made it into Dereham to start his shift. He briefed his constables and sent them off to do their patrols and enquiries. That done he went back to the sergeants' office and started to go through his in-tray. It was just routine stuff, and he soon had it cleared.

He thought back to the events of the previous evening. The fact that Mashrani was planning to kill Mo when they had finished with him, put a completely different light on everything. It was no good getting his police colleagues involved, these swine should never be put before the courts. No, if anything he had to stop any police officer coming into contact with them. They were tooled up with some formidable fire power, even armed response officers would be in danger from these professional killers. At least Chaim was able to introduce some agents to counter the danger. Whether they were Mossad or Shin Bet, they were as ruthless if not more than their Quds Force opponents. There was a likelihood of at least one person overseeing Mo's house, and there were probably some in the area of the holiday let in Stanfield.

He was amazed at Pat's skills and abilities. She knew her way around the attachments on the missile launchers. That mawther* (*Norfolk dialect for a young woman) is a dark horse, thought Pegg. I'm glad she is on our side. He went over what they had discovered. Mashrani had a small anti-aircraft missile system at his disposal. He had some form of supports for the launchers. There was a remote firing system, initiation of which was likely to be a mobile phone or phones. Thanks to Pat's efforts the remote firing system was now useless. The launchers could still be used manually if the receivers attached to the launchers were removed.

Mashrani would only discover that the launchers were not working, after trying to use them, by which time it would be too late to rectify the problem. Pat had sabotaged five of the launchers, but the sixth one was with Mashrani's group.

It was not known if that had a receiver attached to it. At the moment there was no way of checking it. It had to be assumed that the remote firing device was still in place. It must also be assumed that Marham airfield was the first target of choice, but thanks to Mashrani's blunder, this mission had in all probability been aborted. So on the balance of probabilities, the target had to be at North Wendlesham airfield. He went to the large map of Norfolk fixed to the wall of the corridor outside the sergeants' office. The huge collage consisted of about half a dozen 1:50,000 OS sheets stapled together and fixed to a four by eight-foot sheet of softboard. He located the site of the holiday cottage at Stanfield, and the main runway of the airfield. It was only about three to four miles away. He decided to go into his office again. He closed the door and taking the burner phone Chaim had given him dialled Chaim's number.

"Chaim, it's Archie, I think I've worked out where Mashrani's crew are going to attack. It's the USAF airfield at North Wendlesham. The airbase is only three or four miles from where they are holed up."

"I've come to the same conclusion. I now have assets near to where the holiday cottage is at Stanfield, there is also a presence at Mo's house, and we have Mo's warehouse covered."

"Who are these guys, and who do you really work for?"

"You know that I cannot tell you that. All I will say they will do no harm to you or your colleagues. I'm sure you have a good idea of who we are. I'd be obliged if you keep your thoughts about us to yourself. Now I must go Archie, stuff to do and all that."

Pegg's shift went without a great deal of incident. At four o'clock, after briefing the late shift sergeant, he went home.   Pat greeted him; she had spent most of the morning in bed. Like Pegg she had not got to bed until four o'clock that morning, but unlike him, had the opportunity to have a liein. They discussed what they'd done the previous evening.   "So Pat, how do you know so much about mobile phone remote switching devices?"

"Well I may as well tell you but keep it to yourself. Remember I told you at Sheffield we were doing some stuff for a client, and that it was on hold until we get some more funding?"

"Yes, that's why you've got a bit of leave."

"Correct. Well what we are developing is a universal app. One which can be uploaded onto a phone, tablet, or other device. It will be able to operate with provider's systems, without any further adjustment or adaption. One app for everything. In order to get there we had to research all the switching devices, that are commercially available. So I am an expert I suppose.

"Well you certainly did the business last night. So apart from being a lady of leisure this morning, what else have you been up to?"

"I washed my hair, had some lunch. After which I took Fred out for a walk. We went up to Beetley and came back past the Gressenhall museum. On the way back I got a paper and a few items from the shop."

They talked a bit more, before Pegg went and got changed. Pat prepared an evening meal. Afterwards they watched some television. They had an early night.

CHAPTER 31

At the time Pegg was starting his shift, Mashrani was also starting his day. He was going to take Yusef and Ahmad with him to show where he wanted the Strela system deployed. They took the Polo. Hariri and Azzi were instructed to remain at the cottage and look after the assets that had been brought from Mo's warehouse. As they drove out onto the road to North Wendlesham, they ignored the BT Openreach van which was parked at the side of the road.

Mashrani drove to the lay-by located west of North Wendlesham. Yusef checked his phone, the reception strength showed 4 bars. They got out of the car and walked up the hill and into the small wood. Mashrani pointed out some sites where the launcher stands could be placed. Yusef identified two places which would afford a clear field of fire and marked each of them with a bamboo cane. As they deliberated, a pair of F15s roared overhead and banked away to the north. Yusef confirmed that they should have a good chance of bringing the aircraft down. He looked at his phone, yes a good strong signal, the same strength as that in the lay-by.

"Excellent Yusef, we'll return tomorrow night and place two of the launcher stands here."

Yusef drew a sketch and marked where he wanted the stands to be located.

"How long will it take to fit the launchers to the stands?" "A couple of minutes at the most. We've tested the remote devices, and we must assume that the missile's propellant is okay, as there is no way of testing that without firing the missile itself."

"Right let's go to the place where I think the other two launchers stands should be sited."

As they walked back down the hill back to the lay-by, they ignored the middle -aged walker who was walking up the way that they had come. They took no notice of her casual greeting, they passed her without a word. They returned to the VW, and Mashrani drove back through North Wendlesham and onto the unofficial viewing area at the eastern end of the main runway. It was the same with his previous visit a few days ago, theirs was not the only vehicle parked there. In all there were about a dozen cars and vans, including the burger van. Another vehicle joined them and parked to the left of their position. Its occupant, a geeky looking young man, with a pair of binoculars slung around his neck, and carrying millboard with a notebook clipped to it, got out and walked over to the perimeter fence. Mashrani and Yusef got out of the VW, and slowly strolled out of the viewing area and made their way across the road and onwards past the end of the runway. After walking for about ten minutes, they came across a wooded area. This expanse of vegetation was similar to the one they had encountered at the west end of the airfield, only this time the ground was much more level. They entered the tree line and looked back. The perimeter fence was about four hundred metres away, and the end of the runway was a further hundred metres back from that.

Yusef further identified two places where the launchers could be sited. They were a bit forward from the row of landing approach lights. Yusef told Mashrani that any further back from the identified sites then the heat from the bank of lights could affect the missile in its selection of a heat source. As they were speaking two F15's passed overhead, they were about 300 feet above them, they passed over the perimeter fence, and touched down, a cloud of blue smoke emitting from the undercarriage wheels.

Yusef walked to the first of the two places and lay down, he looked along the path which the two aircraft had flown onto the runway threshold. He marked the position with a bamboo cane, and repeated the procedure with the second position, again marking it with a cane. He checked the signal on his phone, there were four bars, good he thought. They walked back to the viewing area. Yusef sat in the passenger side of the Polo, and checked his phone, again the reception showed four bars.

"The phone signal at each end of the runway is very good," said Yusef.

"Have you tried out the initiation sequence of the missiles in an actual live run, using a mobile phone?" asked Mashrani.

Yusef sighed, "Sir we have practised the entire operating procedure before we came over to England, and we checked every part of the switching devices whilst we were down in the unit at Reydon. It will work.".

"I'm glad to hear that Yusef, but even if everything works, do you see any other problems?"

"No. As long as the positioning of the launchers and their stands is done correctly it will be fine. But although we have programmed the speed dialling into the phones, there will be a slight pause before the triggers on the launchers operate. The operator firing the missile will need to be
aware of this."

"So what is the delay."

"It is about on average around about five seconds."

168

"Will that be a problem?"

"Not really, we have the advantage of knowing where the targets are coming from, and we know the flight path of the targets. In a wartime scenario, hostiles could be approaching from any direction. In that case the firer would have to hold and fire the launcher when and where he could acquire a target."

As they were speaking they saw another pair of jets preparing to land. The jets lined up and started their final approach.

"Right," Yusef said, "I dial now, one thousand and one, one thousand and two, one thousand and three, one thousand and four, one thousand and five, missile away!" The jets were just short of the perimeter fence. "The Strelas should catch them just before they touch down."

"Where should the firer be?"

"Firers I would suggest, both launchers need to be activated simultaneously, with luck each missile will acquire a different target. They will be far enough away not to be in danger from debris. You need to remember at this end of the runway, the returning aircraft will have less fuel on board, but at the other end aircraft taking off would normally have a full load. But in that case our firers will be a safe distance away."

"Right Yusef, I think it is time to get all our assets up to the holiday cottage."

"Who is going to do that, one of us or the others?"

"No none of them, I'm going to get our own Mr Shaqaz to do it. Once he has driven the DAF van and delivered the assets to us then we can dispose of him, be rid of him forever."

Mashrani dialled a number.

"Hello, Shaqaz, we need you to take our DAF van to where we are currently staying. I want you to come to us at four o'clock. I will send one of my guys in the Polo. All you have to do is follow him and he will lead you to us."

"I have not got the keys to the van."

"I know you fool, that is why my guy is coming down. As well as leading you back to us he'll give you a set of keys for the DAF."

"How will I get back to Dereham?"

"I'm sick of your questions we'll sort that out when you get to our place. Now if you value your parent's welfare you just do what I say. Four at your warehouse, be there!" Masrani ended the call.

They both sat in the car and said nothing. The viewing area only had two other cars and the burger van parked up on it. One was that of the geek, who was looking through his binoculars, and recording tail numbers of the returning aircraft as they touched down onto the runway.

"I plan to carry out our mission tomorrow. Before we do that, I need to have the stands for the launchers, the launchers, and the missiles in place tonight."

* * *

The BT Openreach van driver looked at the laptop on his knees. He picked up his phone and hit the speed dial: "One of the target vehicles is on the move, it's the VW Polo, and it's heading towards my position."

"Good, monitor it I want to know where it is heading."

The van driver acknowledged and ended the call. He waited until the Polo had passed the van before he said:

"Okay they've gone you can sit up now."

"I'm glad of that I was getting cramp," said a middleaged woman, getting up and settling into the passenger seat.

The driver gave her the laptop he pointed to the screen which displayed a Google Street View map, he pointed to a red flashing star:

"That's the Polo, and we are here, let's see where they are going to."

After twenty minutes the woman said:

"The car is stationary, it's west of North Wendlesham." The driver continued through the village, and after a bit came across the Polo parked in a lay-by, he drove past it, noting that there was nobody in the car. He turned the van around and drove a bit further towards the village. He stopped near a telegraph pole under which was a BT cable box. From where the van was parked the driver had line of sight onto the Polo.

"Right time to do your rambling bit, Ruth. I'll be here working on this box."

His passenger got out of the van and put on a rucksack and started to walk towards the lay-by. Meanwhile the driver took out a toolbox and a folding stool from the back of the van. He went to the cable box, opened the cover, and commenced "working" on the inside of the box.

The woman arrived at the lay-by and took the turning which led onto the public footpath and up the hill. After a while she saw Mashrani, Yusef and Ahmad walking towards her. As they approached her she said:

"Good morning, it's a nice day isn't it?"

The three men ignored her and walked past her saying nothing.

"Sociable bunch of bastards aren't you," she thought and continued along the path. Once she got to the wood, she did a quick appraisal and started to work out where missiles may be launched from. Eban had briefed the team as to how the missiles would be launched, it was just a matter of finding where the launchers would be placed.

After ten minutes she found the first of Yusef's bamboo canes. She photographed it and the immediate surrounds, another five minutes passed, and she located the second cane, and again she took photographs. She returned to the BT Openreach van. The driver packed up his tools and secured the cable box. He put all the kit into the back of the van. He joined the woman in the front. They looked at the Street View image on the laptop, the Polo had travelled through North Wendlesham and was heading east. They saw that the car had driven to a place near to the eastern part of the airfield and had come to a stop. The driver picked up his phone a speed dialled another number:

"Abe they have stopped near to the end of eastern end of the runway."

"Got it on my screen, it's the viewing area if I'm not mistaken, I should be there in a couple of minutes. I'll be doing my plane spotter thing."

Abe, (the geeky young man), drove onto the viewing area, and parked to the right of the Polo. He saw that the occupants of the car had not moved from the vehicle. He put a pair of binoculars around his neck and took a millboard on which he had clipped an open notebook, that done he got out of his car. He walked over to the edge of the viewing area and stood right next to the perimeter fence. He peered through his binoculars and made what appeared to be notes. Out of the corner of his eye he saw the occupants of the Polo get out of the car and walk out of the viewing area. He waited until they had crossed the road, before changing his position. As he did so, a pair of F15s taxied over to the threshold of the runway. They paused before racing down the runway at full throttle and lifting into the air.

He waited until the noise died away before observing the pair from the Polo through his binoculars. He had a good view of what they were up to. They had stopped short of the final row of elevated landing lights. One of them was crouching down out of view before standing up again. He then took a bamboo cane and stuck it into the ground. The three moved to a different position, where the whole procedure as repeated. The one who had crouched down took a notebook from his jacket ant wrote something in it. They all walked back to the viewing area. Abe resumed his position by the fence and continued to play the plane spotter.

The Polo left the viewing area. He phoned the BT Openreach driver:

"They've left my end; I'm going to check out the area they have just left."

"Thanks Abe, we've got them on the Street View, catch you later."

Abe left his position by the fence and walked out of the viewing area, to where he had seen the occupants of the Polo nosing around. He found the two bamboo canes and photographed them and the immediate area around each of them. When he got back to his car, he sent an email with the photographs he had taken to Eban.

CHAPTER 32

Mo was terrified, Mashrani had abruptly ended the telephone call, demanding that he drive the DAF to where Mashrani and his thugs were ensconced. Is this where he kills me he thought to himself. It was lunchtime so it was around four hours before he had to drive the DAF. He called Eban, and explained what Mashrani had told him: "I'm so frightened Chaim, I'm sure these swine are going to murder me, what are we going to do, oh dear God help me!"

"Mo, we've got your back, this may turn out to our advantage, if you'll excuse me for saying that. Right where are you at the moment?"

"At my shop in Dereham."

"Meet me at your warehouse at two. We've got a lot to do."

Chaim ended the call, next he made a couple of more calls, Including one to Pegg.

"Archie it looks like we are approaching the endgame, are you on duty?"

"Day shift, I finish a four, what's happening?"

Eban explained about the call he had just had from Mo, and what he was going to do. He said that by the end of the evening Mo should have his warehouse back. He said that it would be best that Pegg keep away from both the warehouse and the place at Stanfield. He would call at Pegg's house at eight. Could Pegg let him know if that was not possible.

At two o'clock Eban met Mo at the warehouse. Mo was in a dreadful state, and it took all of Eban's powers of persuasion to settle him down. Before he went any further, he got Mo to turn off the CCTV system. He instructed Mo not to turn it on again until the following morning. He then said:

"Let's be clear, Mo, you are not going to drive the DAF to Mashrani's holiday cottage. Once I've briefed you as to what's going to happen. As far as you're concerned your involvement is over, and you can have your warehouse back for you to use as it was intended. After I have told you to leave, there is stuff we need to do, and when we have done, this place will be forensically swept and cleaned, they'll be no trace of either my people or Mashrani's gang of reprobates."

"How are you going to get that done, and how is the van going to get to Mashrani without me with it?"

"It's best you do not ask any more questions. Now give me the keys to the warehouse I'll put them through your shops letter box when I am finished with them. I want you to leave your car parked where it is. Mashrani's crew have to think that you are here inside when they come." Mo gave him the keys to the warehouse.

"Do you want my car keys as well?"

"No but I would like the code for the alarm, we'll arm it when we leave."

Mo wrote it down and gave it to him.

"I'll give Archie a full resume of what we have done and achieved, I've no doubt that he will put you in the picture. I am grateful for all you have done for me. Without you, Archie, and Pat we could not have done it. Give my regards to Muna and Darius and say goodbye to Esi. Now leave and carry on with your life"

After embracing Eban, Mo left and caught a bus back to his shop.

Eban made a phone call:

"I want you both at Mo's warehouse now, tell the others to be on standby to come here as well.

*   *   *

At the holiday cottage in Stanfield Mashrani put the phone back in his pocket, the whole team were gathered in the living room.

"Right Shaqaz will meet Kaled and Ahmad, at the warehouse, take the Polo. He will be driving the DAF, one of you will sit in the van with him. When you get back here, I want him dealt with straight away. Have you dug that hole for the body?"

"Yes it is done," replied Kaled.

"Remember to fit a suppressor onto the weapon you are going to use, we don't want gunshots bringing unwanted attention."

"Now I am going to explain what is going to happen, as I have already told Yusef, we are going to execute our mission tomorrow. Tonight we are going to site the stands and the launchers, each with a missile fitted to it. When we have done that we come back here."

Mashrani spread out the map showing the locations of the sites which he and Yusef had previously selected. "We'll drive the DAF to the lay-by here, and we'll carry two stands, two Strelas and two launchers to each of the sites which have been selected by Yusef and Ahmad. We should be able to carry all the stuff from the van between the five of us in one go.'

175

'When we've done that we will drive to the viewing area at the other end of the airfield. We have to be a bit more careful, as we are much closer to the runway. We will do the same thing, that is site the stands, launchers and missiles, two of each item."

'Yusef and Kaled you will man the site at the western end of the airfield. You will have the Ford van, you will remain at the lay-by, and activate the launchers from your van.'   'Ahmad and Naji, you will drive the DAF to the viewing area at the other end. You will activate the launchers from the vehicle. All of you need to be aware, once you have a target, there will be a delay, between the telephone receiving unit getting the call and its operating of the trigger on the launcher. Yusef informs me it is about five seconds. Remember this when acquiring targets. We'll leave here at midnight. God willing all the stuff should be in place by two. We come back here and grab a few hours' sleep. Tomorrow we need to be in our respective positions by eight o'clock. Once flying starts, we wait until we get aircraft taking off and landing. Any questions?"

"What about the rest of the Strelas?"

"I don't think we can launch any more missiles than the four we'll put in place tonight. I expect that the Yanks will be on the alert after we have let the Strelas off. So we'll leave the spare missiles together with the spare launchers on the back of the DAF. After the attack, we'll return here, and lay low for a day or two. If we have an opportunity to carry out another attack, we'll do so. If not then I have an exit plan for you, to get you back home. I'll explain that when
we have finished the operation tomorrow."

"If you don't mind sir, I'd like to take a couple of Strelas and the spare launcher that we've got here, I need to check a couple of things out. I'll take the Ford, there's a secluded beet pad about a couple of miles away" said Yusef.

"You do what you've got to do, just be careful, I don't want this mission put in jeopardy before it has even started," replied Mashrani.

"I'll be fine boss."

Mashrani looked at his watch:

"Right Kaled and Ahmad, time to get going."

Kaled took the keys to the Polo and accompanied by Ahmad drove off to Dereham. Yusef got the keys to the Ford van, and with the help of Naji, loaded up the launcher and two missiles into the back. He had some blue plastic sheeting which he used to cover the missiles and launcher. He then drove off to the remote beet pad, there he proceeded to run through the operating drills for the SA7 system. The harvested sugar beet stood about three metres high, the pile was "L" shaped. It offered excellent cover from any snooping eyes.

A small single engine plane crossed over travelling south. Yusef aimed at the aircraft. He was fortunate there was quite a bit of air traffic about, a helicopter and an airliner flew over in quick succession. He was not comfortable with the remote firing system that had been decided on to initiate the missiles. He would have been much happier with firers using the system manually. Still the Iranians were calling the shots so there was little he could do. But he would try and persuade Mashrani to have someone as a backup in case the remote system failed.

Another reason he wanted to be away was the planned murder of Shaqaz. He did not like cold blooded murder. Killing those who could fight back is different. It was a subject which put him at loggerheads with the other three of his countrymen. He did not have the say so on who was to come on this operation. He felt he was selected because of his expertise. He would never have selected the others, especially Kaled and Naji, they are more criminals than warriors. He looked at his watch, it was getting on for four o'clock. He would remain until five. That way he'd miss the killing. If it were Kaled pulling the trigger, the evil bastard would enjoy it.

CHAPTER 33

Eban was joined by his colleagues at the warehouse. He had his laptop open on the table in the building's office. The locater app showed that both the other vehicles were still at the cottage in Stanfield. He designated one of the colleagues to monitor it. He gathered the rest of them in the main body of the warehouse.

"Friends," he said, "we are coming towards the climax of the first part of our mission. I am sorry that things have been a bit rushed, I would have preferred more time to prepare, but we are where we are. Now Mashrani is planning an attack on the USAF base at North Wendlesham. He plans to bring down aircraft using missiles. The pieces of kit he will be using are familiar to IDF airmen. The SA 7 Grail system, not the most modern of antiaircraft ordnance, but deadly if used correctly. In the back of the van, are four launchers, and missiles. We believe that a fifth launcher, and two more missiles are unaccounted for. They are probably with Masrani's group at a holiday cottage at
Stanfield.'

'Mo was to meet up with one of Mashrani's group here at four o'clock., and he was to drive the DAF to Stanfield, where Mashrani plans to murder him. We have stopped that from happening, because our own people will be delivering the van to Mashrani. I plan to capture the lot of them and have them sent back to be interrogated by our own people. We will only use lethal force as a last resort."

Eban's briefing was interrupted by the person monitoring the locater app on the laptop, calling from the office:

"Boss, one of their vehicles is on the move." Eban walked into the office:

"Where is it going, it looks as if it's the Ford van?"

179

"It's heading north from the cottage."

"Well it's not coming here, keep an eye on it and find out where it's travelling to," said Eban and started to walk back to the main body of the warehouse, when the person at the laptop exclaimed:

"Wait there is more movement, the Polo is on the move, and heading south!"

"Game on, we've got about twenty minutes, before they are here."

He went back and joined the rest and briefed them as to what was going to happen, they took their positions and waited.

* * *

Kaled and Ahmad left the cottage, Kaled was driving. He was getting quite excited about dealing with Mo.

"Why did Yusef take off like that?"

"He's a moody bastard, I don't like him, I think he's too soft. He talks about being a noble warrior, well I believe you have to be hard and without feelings to do our jobs. And we should be able to have a few perks and earn a bit on the side. People smuggling and hostage taking are nice little earners back home. That wimp Yusef says it is all wrong.

Bah I'm sick of his "noble warrior" stuff. There'll be a reckoning when we're back home, you wait and see Ahmad."

Ahmad said nothing. They drove on. Twenty-five minutes later they were pulling up outside the warehouse.

"I see the little poof is here already, that's his car. I can't wait to slot him when we get back," said Kaled.

"Just leave it, will you, let's get the van back to Stanfield."

Kaled was first out of the car, he went to the door, tried it, it was locked, he thumped with the palm of his hand. There was a pause of a few seconds and the door was opened, Kaled entered, closely followed by Ahmad. That was the last thing either of them remembered. Kaled was pulled through the door, a syringe was plunged into his neck, and he collapsed to the floor. Ahmad had no time to react, before the same thing happened to him. The door was closed and locked. The unconscious men were searched, and the contents of their pockets were placed on the floor beside them. The keys to the DAF were given to one of Eban's operatives.

"Get the back opened. We need to do a quick count of what we have on board, after that open the roller door and get the van out." He said to another one, "Once the DAF is out drive your vehicle in. Come on guys, chop, chop, the clock is ticking."

The operatives rapidly went about their immediate allotted tasks, and after ten minutes they were ready to leave. Two of them were in the front of the DAF, one was driving Khaled's Polo, the third vehicle was a white unmarked Mercedes Sprinter van. There were three operatives in the front, and in the back were a further two operatives, and the unconscious Lebanese, both of whom had their arms and legs restrained with cable ties. They also had gaffer tape over their mouths and black hoods over their heads.

Eban remained in the warehouse, supervising another two operatives who were forensically cleansing the warehouse. By the time they had completed the operation, there would be nothing to link Pegg, Pat, Eban and his operatives as well as Mashrani's crew to the premises.

* * *

At the same time as Eban met Mo at the warehouse, an Antonov An-26, cargo carrier landed at Norwich International Airport. The aircraft was operated by an East European company, The Twin engine turboprop was chartered by an offshore company registered in the Isle of Man. It was due to collect some crates of machine parts and fly them to Tirana, the capital of Albania. The plane had a crew of three, all of them South Africans. The load capacity was 5500 kg, the weight of the load would be well short of this figure.

The captain taxied over to the small cargo terminal, where its cargo of post and parcels were offloaded. The captain and his first officer went to the aircrew rest facility, whilst the loadmaster supervised the re-fuelling of their aircraft. That done, he joined the other crew members.

CHAPTER 34

The three-vehicle convoy made its way to the holiday cottage at Stanfield. It was led by the Polo, followed by the DAF, with the Sprinter in rear position. As they went into Back Lane, the vehicles closed right up. Just prior to the turning into the entrance to the driveway, they stopped and two of the occupants in the front of the Sprinter jumped out and waited at the entrance, hidden from the house by the leylandii hedge. The Polo drove in followed by the DAF. The occupants of the vehicles got out and rapidly fanned out. Mashrani and Naji came out of the door, both of them were overpowered, they were rendered unconscious and trussed up within seconds. The Sprinter drove in and parked next to the DAF. Mashrani and Naji joined Kaled and Ahmad in the back of the Sprinter.

Eban's team searched the cottage, when they had finished, a phone call was made to Eban.

"We've got four of them, but the Ford van is not here. We have also searched the cottage, and we have found a lot of documents, maps and stuff like that, in addition we've got the four M16 rifles a mass of ammo, and four pistols, but we appear to be a launcher and two missiles adrift."

"Right I'm looking at the locater, the Ford van is about a mile or so to the north of you. It would appear that Yusef is loose with a launcher and a couple of missiles. Okay this is what I want you to do."

Ten minutes later the operatives left the holiday cottage in the Sprinter and the Polo together with their four unconscious captives, mobile phones and documents, and maps found in the house and stuff recovered from the captives themselves. The DAF had been left behind at the cottage, together with all the weaponry, ammunition, launchers, and the rest of the missiles. They travelled towards Norwich and when they got to Hellesden, they drove onto an industrial estate and went to a unit which already had its roller door open. The Sprinter van drove in and the roller door was closed behind it. The Polo was driven away and parked up on the Mile Cross estate. There the driver wiped the inside of the car clean, and leaving the keys on the driver's seat, abandoned the vehicle and caught a bus back to Hellesden where he joined the others at the unit.

* * *

When he had finished at the warehouse, Eban told the two people who had cleared up the building to make their way to the industrial unit at Hellesden. He armed the burglar alarm and secured the building.

He took out the burner phone and called Pegg on a likewise device. He briefly explained what had happened. He told him what he was going to do, and he would explain in more detail of what had occurred when he saw him that evening.

The next call was a 999 call to the police control room.

"Norfolk police, what is the nature of your emergency?" "This probably sounds far-fetched, but I suggest you get an armed response team to Back Lane in Stanfield NR20 4HT. There is a white DAF box van registration number," he gave the call taker the number before continuing, "the keys to the van are under a brick next to a water butt at the left side of the house. In the back of the van which is locked there is a considerable amount of weaponry and antiaircraft ordnance. Get there now before someone else does. I am not repeating this as I know you have a recording."

Before the call taker had a chance to respond, Eban had hung up, and after switching the phone off he removed the sim card and drove away.

At the control room the duty inspector wasted no time in dispatching an armed response vehicle (ARV) to Stanfield, an additional one was dispatched shortly after it became available. The first ARV arrived at the cottage twenty minutes later, joined by the other unit ten minutes after that. The keys to the DAF had been located by the first officers on the scene. After checking the immediate area for any form of explosive devices, they opened the back of the van.

The first thing that caught their eye were the assault rifles and pistols. The ARV crewmen from the first vehicle, had now been joined by their colleagues in the second vehicle. The officers exchanged expletives at the shocking discovery. The ARV crewman from the first car called the control room.

"VK we have a serious situation here; we need search and forensics teams here now. We have firearms and a large quantity of ammunition, and further ordnance we can't identify."

"Secure the area and we'll get you some assistance." The control room tried to trace the caller who had informed the police about the DAF van. It was a pointless exercise, neither the caller nor the device could be identified.

* * *

Yusef looked at his watch, it was now gone past fivethirty. He decided to pack up the launcher and missile, and head back to the cottage. That sadistic shit Harari had already killed the poor little Iranian and buried the result of his handiwork. Mashrani would be wondering where he had got to. As he put the missile and its launcher into the back of the van, he heard the sound of sirens in the distance, it got nearer and then it stopped. It

185

was probably some sort of traffic incident he thought as he got into the van and drove off the beet pad. He made his way back to the cottage. As he approached the cottage he saw a police officer standing in the driveway. The officer was cradling what seemed to be a sub machine gun across his chest. He decided to continue to drive towards the cottage, if he stopped and tried to turn around, he would only rouse the officer' suspicions, he drove on and gave the officer a wave. The officer impatiently waved him on. Yusef continued, he glanced inside the driveway and saw that there were at least two other marked police vehicles inside the driveway. What's happened to Mashrani and the others, Yusef thought to himself. How did we get so compromised? Has somebody has betrayed us. I must try and salvage something from this debacle. He decided to find a place to hide up, and tomorrow he would find targets for the two missiles. He drove to the viewing area at the side of the airfield. He found a bit of a hiding place for the van in amongst some gorse bushes. He parked up and cut some branches and covered the vehicle. It was fortunate that the van was green, it was now reasonably camouflaged. It appeared that flying had ceased for the day. As a result there were no vehicles parked in the viewing area. Leaving the camouflaged van and its deadly contents, he walked around the wooded area at the end of the eastern section of the runway.

He noticed that the canes he'd placed earlier that day were still in place. He left them undisturbed. He located a place some five hundred metres further away to the east. It was an area covered with gorse. The vegetation was about shoulder height for Yusef, head height for the average person. The back blast from the launched missile should not ignite the surrounding grass and scrub. He should be able to get both missiles launched without incinerating himself. He walked back to where he had hidden the van. It would be a long wait. He decided to call

Mashrani to see what had happened. He dialled the number:

"*Allo Yusef*" a male voice said.

Replying in Arabic Yusef said," It's all gone to shit boss. Police are swarming all over the cottage where are you and the others?"

"More to the point where are you and what are you doing?"

"You're not Mashrani, who are you?"

"Your friends; tell us where you are, and we'll get you and take you to a safe place."

Yusef ended the call. It was somebody using Mashrani's phone, and not Mashrani that he was speaking to. Maybe it was one of the police. Yusef switched off his phone and removed the sim card. He decided to abandon the van and take the launcher and the two missiles with him.

He'd find somewhere to hide up until the morning.

* * *

At Hellesden the Mercedes Sprinter van drove out of the unit and made its way along the Norwich Ring Road towards the airport. In the back of the van were four wooden crates, stencilled on them were the logo of a well-known Norfolk based engineering enterprise. The accompanying paperwork for the customs manifest stated that the contents were machine parts for Tirana in Albania.

The van made its way to the air freight terminal, where it pulled up beside the Antonov freighter. The aircraft's back ramp already down. The crates were quickly taken aboard and secured in the cargo bay. Four of Eban's operatives remained with the aircraft, the rest left the airport in the Sprinter van.

The four operatives took their place in the dozen or so crew-seats at the front of the cargo bay. The loadmaster closed the loading ramp, and the captain started up the engines. The Antonov taxied out of its slot on the servicing apron and out onto the airfield. Five minutes later it was airborne and a few minutes after that was crossing the Norfolk coast.

The operatives opened the crates and one by one the now conscious occupants were lifted out and carried over to the crew-seats. Their hoods and gags were removed, but the restraints around their wrists and ankles remained in place. The operatives could not hear the captives' protestations, mainly because they were wearing earmuffs, and secondly because of the din in the cargo bay. Instead they gave them water and some sandwiches. The aircraft droned on, and four hours later it touched down at Tirana airport, where it taxied to a remote part of airfield. The operatives transferred the captives to a Jetstream and joined them on board.. The sleek jet left Tirana and three hours later the aircraft touched down at a military airfield near Tel Aviv.

CHAPTER 35

Pegg had finished work and was back home when the first of the police units arrived at the holiday cottage at Stanfield. He still had the burner phone which Eban had given him. He was worried about the missing Lebanese and the missiles and launcher. He decided to try and locate the vehicle the missing Lebanese was using.

"Pat, you've got that locater app Eban gave us on your iPhone."

"Yes, I'll fire up my device," she paused, "here we go. Yes now I've got the van at Stansfield, wait…. the Polo is parked up in Norwich, Mile cross Lane. Let's see, it's searching... got it! The Ford Connect van is stationary, near to the east end of North Wendlesham's runway. I'll zoom in. There's some sort of parking area and it seems to be parked amongst some trees or bushes. Here look." Pegg took the device and looked at the screen.

"It's parked a little bit away from the viewing area. Right Pat I'm going to use the burner which Chaim gave us, and I am going to make an anonymous call to our control room." He gave the iPhone back to Pat and took out the burner, and dialled 999, he held a handkerchief over his mouth as he spoke:

"You need to get some armed units to the public viewing area at the eastern end of North Wendlesham air base. There is a green Ford Connect van. The driver is Yusef al Haddad. He is a Lebanese national, he is armed and in possession of a hand-held anti-aircraft missile launcher." Pegg ended the call and switched off the phone and took the sim card out.

"I hate doing that to my own people, but if I gave my details I'd be in the soft and smelly big time. Especially after what we've been up to for the past few days."

"We did what we had to do, Archie. We've done nothing wrong, and we have taken a lot of bad guys off the street. So stop beating yourself up about it. The only people who know what we have done are Chaim, Mo, me, and you, oh and of course Chaim's lot. I don't suppose they'll be dobbing us in it any time soon. Let's have something to eat and then we wait for what Chaim has to tell us."

* * *

It had started to rain, Yusef was getting cold and wet. He returned to the place where he was going to launch the missiles. As he walked around the area, he noticed the top of a fire tower, about a quarter of a mile away. He made his way towards the structure. It was awkward going, the launcher and the missile had no carrying straps. He eventually made it to the base of the tower. He was now in a fire break, which divided two sections of a conifer plantation.

The tower was constructed entirely from timber. The four legs each consisted of what seemed a single length of wood, running from the ground to where its upper end connected to the roof. If he had looked closer each upright was in three sections, separated by the middle and top parts of the tower. The sides were braced by diagonals. It looked like one of those guard towers at a prison camp. He saw that the height from the ground to the platform was around ten metres. The structure appeared to be a bit rickety. A sign at the base read *"DO NOT CLIMB. UNSAFE STRUCTURE."* Yusef tried the bottom braces, it seemed solid enough. He decided to risk it, at least it would give him some shelter from the rain, which was falling with greater intensity. The ladder from the bottom, led to an intermediate platform, from which another ladder led up to the uppermost platform. He took the spare missile, and climbed the ladder to the middle platform, the ladder creaked but it did not give way. He placed the missile on the wooden surface of the platform and descended to the ground. He retrieved the launcher with the missile attached and climbed up to the middle platform again.

He laid the missiles and launcher down on the floor of the middle platform and climbed up to the top of the structure. Access to the top part of the tower was afforded by an open trap door. Yusef climbed up into the top. Around all four sides were five feet tongued and grooved panels. The gap between the top of the panels to the bottom edge of the roof was four feet.

Yusef looked out he had an all-round view of the immediate area. He could see the end of the runway about half a mile away. He thought to himself this would be an ideal location to launch the missiles. The inside of the top platform was reasonably sheltered from the rain, which had eased somewhat. It was getting dark; he fetched the launcher and the two missiles. It would be cold, but a least he was dry. He remained where he was and waited until daybreak.

CHAPTER 36

Eban arrived at Pegg's house a few minutes after eight o'clock. Pegg and Pat had already eaten. Eban declined an offer of some food. Pegg made some coffee and they sat in the living room. Eban gave a complete debrief on the day's events.

"What we have achieved today went beyond my wildest expectations. To be candid, I thought we may have had a blood bath on our hands. As it was we captured most of Mashrani's group, without any injury or loss of life."

"There is still the one Lebanese outstanding," said Pegg. "Yes, Yusef al Haddad, for some reason he was not at the holiday cottage with Mashrani and Naji bin Azzi. It was too late to change our plan. I had to get the captives out of the country."

"Where are they now?"

"I'm afraid I can't tell you, but they will be interrogated at a secure location. Any information we get from them, we'll pass it on the security services in this country."

"Are they going to go before some court.?"

"Yes. The four Lebanese are suspected of murder, kidnap, and people smuggling. Mashrani is a different matter. He is a serving officer in the IRGC Quds Force, there is a lot of stuff we need to find out. We suspect he is one of a number of operatives who have gone rogue. The Islamic Republic of Iran is a radical regime; however the top people would not sanction an operation like this."

"Why wouldn't they," asked Pat?

"It is against their interests. Whilst relations with many west European countries are somewhat strained. The regime will not gain anything by exacerbating a difficult state of affairs."

"We have been told that there are factions within Iran who feel that the government is not radical enough," said Pegg.

"There are indeed, if these groups should prevail things will get even more unstable than they currently are in the Middle East and beyond. But what we have done will go a long way to mitigate the risk of this happening. The three of you have done a fantastic job, we could not have done it without you.'

'Mo told Archie about the threat to Mo's parents. You Archie used your own resources without getting any of the law enforcement or security agencies involved. This would have undoubtedly put the lives of Darius, Muna and Mo in danger.'

'You gave us images of the team from Lebanon, which we were able to put names to. And you Pat! What can I say? You put those four launchers out of commission by disabling the remote firing devices. Although in the end it did not matter, but if things had worked out differently, we would have been in serious trouble. Thank you for that."

"I was glad I could use some of my expertise to assist in the operation," Pat said.

Eban continued, "We have the name of the IRGC officer masquerading as an agricultural attaché at Iran's London embassy, what he did too, plus the telephone evidence of his conversations with Mashrani, I have his phone by the way, will be passed onto the Foreign Office, I've no doubt he will be on his way back to Teheran in the very near future We have all the others in the bag with the exception of Haddad. I don't think I can do much to help you there at the moment."

"There's no need," said Pegg, "I anonymously let my people know the whereabouts of the green Ford Connect van. The transponder was still working, and Pat was able to get its location using the app on her iPhone.

"So what's happening then?" asked Eban.

"I basically said Haddad was near the public viewing area at North Wendlesham airfield, with a launcher and two missiles."

"Well if they get him, there is nothing to connect my people or yourselves to him. Now if you don't mind, I'll take those burner phones from you, and can you erase that locater app from your smart phones as well?"

"What about the transponders, can they be liked to your organisation?"

"They are available on the commercial market we obtained them from a company in London, they sell thousands and thousands of them each year. Don't worry they'll not be traced back to either us or you!"

They talked more about what they had achieved. Eban was going to go back to Cambridge, where he would resume his role as a visiting lecturer. Pat, Pegg, and Mo would not hear from Chaim Eban again. He left Pegg's house at ten.

Pegg had an early shift to do in the morning, after which he would take a few days off, or so he thought.

* * *

When the control room received Pegg's anonymous call, units were deployed to North Wendlesham. It was not long before the Ford Connect van was located. It had been raining quite hard and it was getting dark. A dog was involved in the search of the immediate area. Efforts to locate the occupant of the van had proved fruitless. The ground was saturated and the presence of wildlife, especially rabbits, had eradicated any useful scent. The van was recovered to a police pound in order for a detailed forensic examination of the vehicle to be carried out.

CHAPTER 37

Major Tom O'Brien had an early morning training mission. He had a new WSO, who had just arrived at North Wendlesham, the airman was a member of the Indiana Air National Guard and was on a temporary attachment to the station. The aim of the mission was to fly to the nearby bombing range at RAF Holbeach and let the ANG crewman practice using the weapons system. The F15 Eagle was going to be the only aircraft flying that morning. The aircraft was loaded with four practice bombs on both wing pods. The bombs were inert, and had no laser guided technology, they were freefall ordnance. Much cheaper than using the genuine article.

He taxied the aircraft from its Hardened Air Shelter (HAS) and onto the taxiway. O'Brien's crew chief had wanted the engines to be given a full workout. So after their visit to the bomb range, they would fly out over the Wash and to the North Sea, where the fighter would be taken up to its maximum speed, by using the re-heat facility to boost the engines to maximum power.

O'Brien halted the aircraft at the "09" threshold. He waited for the control tower to give permission to go. The order was received, and O'Brien pushed the throttles fully open. The F15 raced down the runway and lifted into the air. The village of North Wendlesham came past on the right as O'Brien banked over and headed north.

* * *

Pegg had already briefed the shift. Two of his officers were deployed to the holiday cottage at Stanfield to guard what had become a crime scene. Pegg decided to take a look, he took the patrol sergeant's car. The DAF van had been recovered to the secure police pound where it joined the Ford Connect van. The Polo had also been recovered. Prior to the vehicle's recovery, a young man had been stopped on the Heartsease estate by Norwich officers, he was arrested on suspicion of theft of a motor vehicle. The contents of the DAF van were removed, after an initial examination by a CSI. The rifles, pistols and ammunition were not so much of a problem as the missile launchers and missiles. Expertise was needed to make these items of ordnance safe. As there were armourers at RAF North Wendlesham, a specialist explosive ordnance disposal (EOD) section was deployed to the holiday cottage. The USAF Master Sergeant in charge of the section was familiar with the SA7 anti-aircraft system, having served in both Iraq and Syria in support of special forces. The senior airman advised that the age of the missiles could mean that both the warhead explosive and propellant were in an unstable condition. He recommended that the missiles should be destroyed rather than disarmed and made safe. His inspection of the small arms ammunition found that these items were not only in date but serviceable.   The Armalite rifles, Glock pistols and the small arms ammunition were taken to the Norfolk Constabulary's Force armoury together with the missile launchers. The missiles were removed by the USAF EOD team and subsequently destroyed.

The CSI officers were still processing the scene when Pegg came to bring the officers who were guarding the scene some food and hot drinks. He told them that he would send someone to relive them at midday.   He went over to one of the CSI's:

"Have you found anything useful?"

"Loads of prints and some DNA from cigarette butts and cups, but as we have no samples to compare at the moment, the samples will have to go on file for now." Peg thought that there was fat chance of matching anything as. With the exception of Haddad, all suspects were out of the country.

"There was one thing though," said the CSI, "at the back of the house there was a freshly excavated area of the garden, which I can only describe as a grave, I don't know if the suspects were planning to murder somebody or not." Pegg feigned surprise. Mo, he thought, I'm so glad we got you out of this whole thing. Pegg said his farewells to the CSI and his two officers. He decided to drive down to where to the green Ford Connect had been found. He drove out of the driveway and into Back Lane. He decided to drive through North Wendlesham and back to the eastern part of the airfield.

There was an explosion in the air above him. Pegg stopped the car and glanced up. A jet was heading towards the village leaving a trail of smoke behind it.

* * *

Yusef was woken up by the roar of jet engines on reheat. He was very cold and was feeling very stiff. He was surprised he had even got to sleep, but he had. He looked at his watch it was just gone eight o'clock, had he slept for that long? He stood up and could see a jet fighter lifting up and banking away in the distance. Yusef cursed, an opportunity missed. He would wait.

* * *

Tom O'Brien lined up the aircraft. Holbeach bombing range had a series of targets for training purposes, amongst them an old trawler. It was on a mudbank, but with the tide being out its hull was completely exposed.

"Your target is coming up an old boat."

197

"I've got it", said the WSO looking at the screen in front of him, "keep it there." O'Brien held the aircraft level.

"Bombs away," he heard in his headphone. O'Brien banked away, "Bulls eye!"

O'Brien glanced down at the boat and two puffs of smoke confirmed that the practice bombs had indeed hit the target.

O'Brien was pleased that the ANG "Wizzo" had succeeded with his first attempt at operating the F15's weapons system.

"Just to show me that wasn't beginner's we'll do it once again. Okay?"   "Ready for that!"

O'Brien took the aircraft around for another pass. He lined the Eagle up and the Wizzo guided them in. The last two bombs were released, and again these hit their target. O'Brien took them out of the range area and over a cloudy North Sea. He opened up the throttle to full extent and took the Eagle to its maximum speed. He remained at that velocity for twenty minutes, before easing back. He decided to give the ANG airman a little taste of the Eagle's performance. He did a few loop the loops and some barrel rolls. He finished with a few sharp turns before saying:

"How're you doing back there?"

"Just fine, my burp bag is still in my pocket."

"Glad about that, you throw up in my airplane you clean it up!"

There was a chuckle in his ear.

"Time to head home fuel's getting low."

O'Brien turned the aircraft south and started the journey back to base. It was not long before the airfield was back in view.

O'Brien made a circuit around the base and was starting to bank to make the final approach.

Just before he was about to put the landing gear down, the incoming missile alarm sounded briefly before there was a thump from the back of the aircraft, a number of warning lights came on. O'Brien tried to maintain control of the damaged aircraft. He operated the mechanism for the rear ejector seat. The canopy blew off and the ANG airman was thrown out of the cockpit still strapped to the rear seat. The jet was headed towards North Wendlesham, O'Brien was aware that the village school was directly in the path of the stricken aircraft. He managed to steer the juddering and yawing machine over the school. The plane bellied into a field of sugar beet. O'Brien's last thought before everything went black was, "What'll happen to June and the twins?"

*   *

*

Yusef's patience was rewarded. He saw the F15 Eagle approaching the airfield. He lined up the already shouldered launcher. As the jet banked Yusef had an excellent view of the rear of it. He aimed at a point directly between the twin tail fins and pressed the trigger. He never knew if the Strela had hit the Eagle.

The back blast from the missile destroyed one of the main supports of the tower. He had not considered that the angle of the launcher was too high, and the corner of the platform was blown to pieces. The rickety structure collapsed. Yusef fell from the tower followed by the launcher and the unfired missile. He hit the ground, breaking his back, the unfired missile fell point first and buried itself in the unconscious man's chest. The rest of the tower collapsed on top of him.

*   *

*

Pegg turned the car around and raced to where he saw the aircraft was heading. The cockpit canopy flew off followed by an ejector seat. Moments after the parachute deployed and floated out of view. Pegg saw the jet belly flop into a beat field before flipping over on its back, coming up again and coming to rest on its side.

Pegg drove the car onto the edge of the field and getting out, raced over to the now broken jet. As he approached he sniffed, the whole area reeked of aviation kerosene. The fumes caused Pegg's eyes to start watering. He went to the front of the plane and could see the unconscious pilot was still strapped in his seat. He took the jack-knife from his stab vest pocket, and slashed through the harness straps, and released the pilot. Pegg heaved, the adrenal rush had given him almost superhuman strength, and he managed to pull him clear. He hoisted the limp body onto his shoulder and made his way away from the wreckage towards his car. A broken lead in the bowels of the ruined F15 started to short circuit and the resulting sparks ignited the kerosene fumes. The aircraft exploded in a fireball. Pegg sheltered the unconscious airman with his body. The pilot escaped any further injury. Pegg was not so lucky Pieces of debris had been blown out of fireball, and Pegg had been struck on the head, and a piece of metal had embedded itself in his back. The last thing he remembered was the jet exploding and after that it was just darkness.

CHAPTER 38

Angie answered her door and found a uniformed superintendent and a sergeant standing on the doorstep.

"Mrs Mason, Mrs Angie Mason?"

"Yes, has something happened?"

"Can we come in?"

Angie let the two officers in and led them into the living room.

"You are Archie Pegg's next of kin, I'm afraid I have some bad news for you, can you sit down." Angie was stunned:

"Not my Archie, no, no!" she gasped, "what has happened?"

"He's been taken to the Norfolk and Norwich, where he has had an operation to ease bleeding on the brain, and he also has a serious injury to his back. We have been informed that he is in a critical condition. I am so sorry Mrs Mason, but we have been told that the prognosis is not good."

Angie slumped down in an armchair:

"What happened?"

"We don't know the precise details, but one of the aircraft from North Wendlesham crashed. Archie pulled the pilot out of the plane before it exploded. The pilot survived, but he was badly hurt, Archie was hit by debris when the aircraft exploded."

The superintendent went on to explain how both the airman and Pegg were taken to the same hospital. The other crew member managed to eject before the plane went in.

"Is there anything we can do, or there someone we can get to sit with you,"

"No my husband is at work, in Norwich, I can give him a call, could you get someone to go to Archie's house, his partner Pat Warrington is there, it would be better if you could get someone to let her know as well. I can't do much more as my daughter can't be left on her own. Once my husband gets here, I can be free to go to the hospital." After a few more minutes the officers left. Catherine Rose was upstairs having a mid-afternoon nap. Angie decided to leave her be. She phoned Ross at his workplace at Norwich airport. She explained what had happened. Ross said he would be home within the hour. She turned on the television and selected the BBC news channel. There was something about a drought in Australia, but her attention was drawn to the news feed ribbon at the bottom of the screen: *Breaking: A US military jet crashes in Norfolk near school, only casualties at this time aircrewman and police officer.* Angie kept the TV on and watched the screen, ignoring any other news report, just watching the newsfeed. Eventually the newsreader changed topic:

"Now we'll go to our local BBC correspondent in Norfolk."

"Yes thank you, I am just as near to the site as I can be, where the jet, a F15 Eagle, crashed. There were two people in the aircraft, one escaped before the plane went in using an ejector seat, he is apparently alright, and is currently at the nearby US Airforce base. The pilot managed to steer the plane away from the local village school, before crashing the aircraft into the field behind me. In an unbelievable feat of bravery, a police officer managed to pull the pilot out of the wreckage before the plane burst into flames. I have just learnt that both the pilot and the officer are in a serious condition at the Norfolk and Norwich hospital."

"Do we know the cause of the crash?"

"Not at the moment. The crash site has been sealed off. Whilst air crash investigators examine the site." *"Thank you for that we'll give more information as and when it comes in. Now for sports news......"*

Angie turned off the television. Twenty minutes later the phone rang.

"Oh Angie," sobbed Pat," I take it you've just heard about Archie?"

"Yes, why don't you come over, Ross will be back soon, and we can take a trip up to the hospital, bring the poodle, we can leave him here."

An hour later they were driving to Norwich.

* * *

A police search team were searching the area east of the airfield, a dog handler was in attendance as well as a pair of armed officers. There had been no further trace of the missing Lebanese Haddad, they had continued the search from the previous evening, when rain had caused the search with dogs off. They came across the collapsed fire tower, as they were starting to examine it, the dog started to get very agitated, it was barking and tried to scramble onto the pile of timber. The handler put the animal on its leash. The firearms officers told the others to back off. One of them issued a challenge:

"Armed police come out!" After issuing the warning three more times, the officer looked into the wrecked structure, he saw a pair of feet poking out from one of the spars. He climbed onto the pile and looked down.

Haddad's lifeless face stared up at him. Then he saw the tail end of the missile protruding from the dead man's chest.

"You can stand everyone down we've got the outstanding person, and he's in no position to hurt anyone. We need to get specialist up here to remove that rocket thing before anything else."

The search team supervisor informed the control room, who delayed the immediate response. Ten minutes later the armed officers were told to remain where they were and preserve the scene. The rest were stood down. An hour later a number of USAF airmen, accompanied by a pair of Norfolk Constabulary Special Branch officers turned up. The Special Branch officers told the two firearms officers to go, and not discuss what they had found.

The USAF personnel, all from RAF North Wendlesham, started the job of processing what was a crime scene, starting with photographs and measurements. A large recovery truck with a crane moved in, and piece by piece the pile of timber was moved from around the body. The missile was extricated and together with the launcher taken away by a pair of armourers. The body was taken to the morgue at the airbase. Two hours later, apart from the timber which had made up the fire tower, every trace of Yusef al Haddad and the missile system had gone. The crash site had been completely sealed off, and the scene had been handed over to a joint RAF/USAF team of investigators. Armed service personnel moved on any sightseers.

* * *

Angie and Pat arrived at the hospital and were directed to the intensive care unit (ICU). They identified themselves to the nurse in charge:

"Mr Pegg is very poorly, and the next few hours will tell how things progress. We have moved some metal from his skull, and there was a larger piece of metal which was removed from his back. His stab vest did take a lot of the impact, which probably saved his life, however there is some damage to his spine."

"Can we see him?" asked Angie.

"We've put him in an induced coma, you'll not get anything out of him, but I'll take you to him. Be warned there are a lot of tubes sticking out of him."

As they made their way to Pegg's bedside, they passed another ICU bed, the patient had an arm and a leg in plaster. His head was bandaged, and he appeared to be asleep or unconscious; sitting beside the bed were a woman and a clergyman in USAF uniform. The woman was red-eyed, and the padre had his arm around her shoulder. She had a rosary in her hand.

They arrived at Pegg's bedside. He was on a ventilator, there were tubes in his mouth, in his nose and a drip attached to his wrist.

"Archie please get better we need you so much," said Angie. "Pat's here as well."

"My darling we are all wishing for the best, keep fighting, don't give up," said Pat.

They sat there and continued to have a conversation with the comatose man. They became aware of the woman who had been sitting with the patient next door, the padre was standing next to her.

"I'm sorry to disturb you, my name is June O'Brien, and that's my husband Tom in there," she started to sob. Pat got up and took her hand:

"He's in good hands here, they'll make him better, don't you worry," she said.

"No it's not that. The man lying in that bed saved my husband's life, if it were not for that hero, my Tom would have died in that airplane."

Angie and Pat said nothing, they looked at Pegg and back to June.

"Tom was the pilot?" asked Angie.

"Yes it was going to be happy day for us. I just heard that we had approval to adopt a pair of twins. Tom did not know,
I just found out and then this happened. But at least there's something to look forward to. How is that brave man doing?"

"The next few hours should see how things turn out," she said.

They spent the next few minutes talking. Angie talked about her daughter, and June showed pictures of the Posetti twins. Eventually they went back to their bedside vigils. The next twenty-four hours would see their lives change forever.

CHAPTER 39

The cause of the destruction of Major Tom O'Brien's aircraft was hushed up. The Board of Inquiry concluded that the F15 Eagle had a major engine failure. Evidence to the contrary was removed and destroyed. The unofficial and top-secret investigation concluded that a Strela missile had struck the starboard engine. Its warhead had failed to detonate but the kinetic energy of the missile had buried itself into the turbofan, ruining, and disrupting control surfaces. The pilot had no chance of flying the aircraft to safety. As it was O'Brien's quick thinking had saved the life of the ANG officer, and by avoiding the school, many other lives were saved as well. The findings of the secret enquiry were filed and in one of the many vaults at the Pentagon, a copy was filed with the Security Service in London, nobody outside the Security Service got to read it.

Yusef al Haddad's remains were interred in a Muslim cemetery in Peterborough, he was buried under an assumed name.

The vehicles which Masrani's team had used were traced to the Fashion Trends warehouse in Nottingham. The premises were raided, and Leila Hosein along with Michael Ali were taken into custody. No further evidence was found to link the pair with Mashrani's plans. They were innocents whose only link to Mashrani was the fact they were his employees engaged in a legitimate business enterprise. They were subsequently released, the vehicles registered to the company were eventually returned.

*　　*

*

The three surviving Lebanese were subsequently put on trial and sentenced to terms of imprisonment for the crimes they had committed.

Mashrani was interrogated at length, it was decided to return him to Iran, as he had not committed any offences against Israel or its citizens. He begged to be allowed to stay. He bargained with his interrogators, he offered details of Al Quds Forces undercover officers in the United Kingdom and beyond. His revelations were forwarded to London and gratefully received by the security services. He was given a new identity, and sent to Australia, where he assisted their security services in identifying rogue elements amongst the Iranian émigré community.   Ali Mochta Ghazi was declared persona non grata and was due to be expelled, but the day before he was due to depart, he walked into London's Paddington Green Police station and asked for asylum. He was whisked away by Special Branch. The information he gave up, filled the gaps left by Mashrani's information. Over the next few months most of the Quds Force clandestine activities, including cyber ops, were rolled up.

In Iran Pejman was not put on trial or arrested, but the information fed by Mossad through unofficial channels, caused him to fall victim to an assassin's bullet. His offshore assets were recovered and paid back to Iran and used for the benefit of that troubled country's people. The fixer in Syria disappeared and was never seen again. His assets in offshore banks were emptied. Medecins sans Frontiere's funds for their work in Syria, Gaza, and Yemen received an enormous boost a short while later.

*   *

*

Leila and Michael decided to take over Fashion Trends officially. They were helped by Afrim Babic to register as directors at Company House. They took on more staff, and now run a very successful business. Babic continued to purchase stock for his own burgeoning enterprises.

*   *

*

Mo's parents had settled well in their adoptive country. Esi had assisted them to apply for settled status. Darius' health had improved so much that he had come off some of the medication. He had developed a close relationship with Esi, who he regards as his "other son." He had found himself a job as a teacher at Norwich City College, temporary at first, and then a permanent post. Muna likewise was able to work as a teacher, she got a job in one of Norwich's girls' school, teaching mathematics and science. The girls adored her; she soon became one of the school's most popular teachers. Her pupils' exam results were testimony to her skills.

Darius and Muna soaked up the culture which Norwich offered. Theatre, concerts, galleries they eagerly drank it all in. They were able to rent a small flat near to the centre of the city. They are currently waiting to apply for UK citizenship.

CHAPTER 40

Three Months Later

"Come on Archie! We need to get going," said Pat.

"Okay, I'm coming just trying to clip this tie on, and then I'm done"

"Come here let me do it," Pat fastened the black neckwear, "let's have a look at you."

She stood back and looked at the man before her. She could not get over the progress he had made since that fateful day when he had been flown to the ICU at the N & N hospital more dead than alive, together with that American airman. He had initially been in a wheelchair, but now just needed a walking stick. He was dressed in his best tunic, the two rows of medal ribbons above the left breast pocket, his boots gleamed. Here was the man they had nearly lost. Helicoptered in together with the American airman he'd rescued to the Norfolk and Norwich Hospital. He was living testimony to the skill and devotion of the air ambulance, surgeons and nursing staff.

"Right she said let's go, Angie, Ross and the baby are waiting in the minibus outside."

"What about the poodle?"

"He's on Angie's lap, now move!"

"You're worse than my old sergeant major sometimes, Miss Warrington!"

She laughed, and led him out to the dark blue minibus, parked on the road outside the house. A young USAF airman, dressed in best blue uniform held the door open, and assisted Pegg into a seat, Pat took a seat beside him. Angie and Ross greeted him. Catherine Rose was sitting between them in a child seat. Fred whined from his perch on Angie's lap.

The airman closed the door, and joined the driver, a likewise clad colleague in the front of the vehicle.

"Are we all secure and belted folks?" the first young airman asked.

A chorus of "Yes" filled the back of the minibus. The van moved off.

The United States Air Force in Europe command (USAFE) had received authority for the Secretary of the Air Force in Washington to award Pegg with a medal for saving the life of Major Tom O'Brien, who had already received the Royal Humane Society's scroll as a result of steering his stricken aircraft away from North Wendlesham primary school. He was also due to be awarded the United States Distinguished Flying Cross. The minibus was waved through the main gate of RAF North Wendlesham, onto a hangar which had "100th Fighter Wing Maintenance Squadron" painted above its vast doors. Three F15 Eagles had been towed out of the hangar and were parked on the apron outside. The vehicle continued through the open doors. The interior had been emptied of its everyday paraphernalia, and in place of it were rows of seating, facing a raised platform. On either side of the dais were a flagpole, one with the Stars and Stripes and the other with the Union Jack. On the dais was a microphone on a stand, behind which were standing three USAF officers, one of whom was a Major General There was a military band, made up of some fifteen musicians, drawn up by the right side of the dais. The seating was some twenty rows deep and thirty rows across. The front row was partially filled, most of the remaining seats were occupied by both uniformed personnel and families.

The minibus stopped by the open doors, the young airman opened the side door, and Pegg's party got out. The driver also got out and took Fred off Angie and put him in on the passenger seat next to the driver. The other airman escorted them to the front of the seating. Pegg walking with the aid of his stick supported by Pat. Ross walked behind them carrying his daughter with Angie by his side. They were shown to their seats. They saw that Tom O'Brien was also seated, with June in the seat next to him.

Guilia Posetti was sat on his lap, and Gino was sitting on June's. Pegg was ushered into the seat next to Tom. The others were seated to right of Pat.

A male voice announced on the PR system:

"All stand please for the anthems of the United Kingdom and the United States."

A young African American woman in USAF uninform stepped from the back of the assembled musicians, microphone in her hand, started to sing God Save the Queen in an exquisite soprano voice, accompanied by the band. Pegg was moved to tears.

She finished and the band paused before playing the Star-Spangled Banner, the soprano sang the first only of the anthem's four verses. Everyone sat down again. The male voice then introduced the Air Force general and the recipients of the awards which were to be presented. Pegg looked along the front row and saw that the Chief Constable. Matt Boggis and Mel Hobson were sitting either side of the chief. All the officers were in uniform. The PR system announced:

"Constables Melanie Hobson and Matthew Boggis please step up to the rostrum."

The young officers stepped up and the general shook each of them by the hand, the PR system continued:

"The actions of this young man and woman saved the lives of the children of the late Mario and Lucia Posetti. They are awarded the USAF Certificate of Meritorious Conduct." The general presented each of them with a framed certificate. He again shook their hands. A photographer took a picture of the officers holding their certificates, standing either side of the general. The hangar erupted in applause and whistles. The pair acknowledged the audience and made their way back to their seats. The PR sounded once more:

"Major Thomas O'Brien, deputy commander 60th Fighter Squadron is awarded the Distinguished Flying Cross. The medal is awarded to any member of the United States Armed services to who distinguishes him or herself by exhibiting extraordinary achievement while participating in aerial flight. Major O'Brien's aircraft suffered catastrophic engine failure. He had seconds to decide whether to abandon the airplane and save himself. If he had taken this course of action the aircraft could have crashed onto our local primary school here at North Wendlesham. He chose to eject his crewman and remain with the airplane. He was seriously injured. The courage of our next person on this rostrum, and the wonderful folks at the Norfolk and Norwich hospital ensured he is able to receive this medal. Major

O'Brien please step up to the rostrum."

Tom got up, put Guilia down on the lap of the woman sitting next to June and made his way to the dais. The general came forward, Tom saluted, and the senior officer returned it. He took the medal from a cushion held by an aide and pinned it on Tom's chest. As he was about to leave the PR system mentioned:

"And another thing O'Brien, you are incorrectly dressed." Tom looked askance as the general took an envelope from inside his jacket and took the microphone.

"I have here some insignia that this officer needs to be wearing. Sort your dress out Lieutenant Colonel O'Brien!"

The rest of the conversation between them was drowned out by the cheers, hoots, whistles and applause. Tom made his way back to his seat. Guilia left the lap she was sitting on and climbed onto Tom's knees she clung to him, her arms around his neck. June kissed him and held his hand.

"Our final award recipient is a person who is not an American, and neither is he a serviceman. He is a police officer whose actions on the day of our Tom O'Brien's air accident were well above what we would expect of any serviceman let alone a civilian police officer. Sergeant Archie Pegg of the Norfolk Constabulary pulled an unconscious Major O'Brien out of the wreckage of his airplane and got him to safety shortly before it exploded. In doing so, he suffered life threatening injuries. It was touch and go whether he would make it, but thanks to the medics he pulled through. The Secretary of the Air Force has authorised the presentation of the United States Civilian Award for Valour. Sergeant Pegg please step up to the rostrum."

Pegg was helped up to the rostrum by the young airman who had ushered them in, he needed a little help to get up the step, the general came forward and took his hand and led him to the centre of the dais. He took a medal from the cushion and pinned to Pegg's tunic lapel. Pegg stepped back, and although he had no headdress on, he saluted the officer. The general returned the salute and led him to the front of the rostrum, where the young airman guided him back to his seat everyone stood up and applauded, the band struck up.

"Oh for he's a jolly good fellow". The hall resounded with cheers and applause."

"Archie," O'Brien said, "we'd like you to come back to our house we got a little party for you, are you up for that?" Pat and Angie chorused:

"You bet he is!"

Fifteen minutes later the minibus arrived at the O'Briens' quarter. It was one of those substantial dwellings built in the nineteen-thirties.

The Posetti twins and Catherine Rose were introduced, and like most kids, it was soon as if they'd known each other all of their little lives, Fred was very pleased to be with the little ones, as the prospect of the children getting food, meant there were bits of food being dropped on the floor, and even better the little people feeding him. A finger buffet had prepared. June called for order:

"I need to explain something for our British guests. When an officer gets a promotion, it's normal for his family to pin the new insignia onto the newly promoted's uniform, heck when Tom got his Captain to Major I did the deed. I'd like to invite our honoured guest Archie to do it instead. Archie Pegg step forward, Colonel up here as well!" Pegg made his way to June, she gave him the envelope the general had given Tom. Tom stood beside Pegg; his gold oakleaf major's badges had been removed from the epaulettes on his jacket. He took the silver oakleaf insignia and fastened them to the airman's jacket. O'Brien embraced Pegg, and the room exploded in cheers and applause, the children shrieked, and Fred barked with excitement.

The party started to break up three hours later. The children had gone to sleep on the large sofa, Fred was clearing up the detritus of their meal from the carpet. After saying their farewells the minibus took them home, first to Swaffham, dropping off Angie, Ross and the baby, before stopping at Pegg's in Gressenhall. The airmen declined Pegg's offer to have some coffee and cake. They saluted Pegg and left.

Pegg and Pat let themselves into the house. He had packed his award into its presentation box along with the citation, Pat had put it in her handbag. He took Pat in his arms and hugged her.

"I do not know how would have coped without you being here."

"I could not have been anywhere else but here. You have done so well. I did not know if I would ever see you again after seeing you in that intensive care ward." She started to cry.

"Hey, come on, I'm here now, not quite the same physically, but in my head I'm still the same man." "I know that. But what is going to happen with the job?" "Well I'm due to go before a medical board at the end of the month. I will make a decision whether to retire or not. They'll probably give me ill health retirement."

"Well I won't mind if I have you to myself, Angie certainly won't be sorry if you hang the uniform up for good."

"Well that's it then. I think my minds made up. Come on, I'm tired let's have an early night sweetheart."

CHAPTER 41

The following day amongst the post were two letters, one was for Pat and the other was for Pegg. Pat opened hers: "It looks as if the department wants me back, you remember that project I was on, and it was put on the back burner?"

"That universal app?"

"That's the one. Well it seems that the client has come up with some dosh, so the research can continue." "You've must go, I'll be fine, I can drive now, my physio sessions have been transferred to the local fitness centre. My next post op appointment is at the end of this month."

"Are you okay with that?"

"Of course! Look Pat, you have been through so much these past few of months. The Uni has been fantastic giving you such a long sabbatical, now is the time to get your life back on track. When do they want you back?

"Next Monday."

"Well that's four days away. Perhaps we could travel back with you.

"We?"

"Me and Fred. I'll find a place to stay near High Bradfield.

"You'll do nothing of the sort. You'll stay with me." "What about your parents.?

"They would love to see you, if you're feeling such a prude about sharing my bed, there is a spare room you know!"

Pegg laughed and gave her a hug.

"Now," she said, "what's your letter about?"

Pegg looked at the back of the envelope. It had the Royal Coat of Arms and "Buckingham Palace" printed on top of the envelope. He opened it:

"From the Lord Chamberlain's Office. It says Dear Mr Pegg, Her Majesty has commanded me to inform you that you are to be awarded the George Medal, for an act of extraordinary bravery, in that you rescued an American airman from certain death. You will be informed at a later date when you will be presented with this award for bravery."

Pegg sat there holding the letter, he said nothing.

"Oh Archie, I'm so proud of you," Pat eventually said. "Well that's something to look forward to. Pat I've got something to tell you. I've been mulling it over since we went to bed, I didn't really sleep much. I'm going to pack it in"

"The police?"

Yes. I am still not quite where I want to be as regards fitness. If I went back to work, I'd only be a liability, and it's not fair to my colleagues. The guvnors have been very understanding about my absence, but they need a decision, and I'm going to give them one." He put the letter away, and took the phone off its base, he paused, looked at Pat and dialled.

"Hello, its sergeant Pegg, could you put me through to the Super?" A minute or so later the superintendent answered:

"Archie how are you doing?"

"Sir, I am getting better all the time, but I feel it is time for me to go."

The Super said nothing for a few moments, before he finally spoke:

"I understand perfectly, we'll all be sorry to see you leave us. You must have given it a lot of thought, before you phoned me. So there is obviously nothing I can say to change your mind. I will pass on your decision to HR at Force Headquarters. You have done the Force proud, Archie, and we'll miss you. I'll see you more formally at a later date. I am so pleased that your courage has been recognised with the award of the George Medal"

"Who put me up for it Sir?"

"I can't say too much, Archie, but all I will say, someone told the Palace!"

The conversation went on for a few more minutes, before Pegg ended the call.

* * *

Pegg had a thorough medical from the Force Medical Officer. The results of this were considered by the medical board which was convened shortly after. The board recommended discharge from the Force on medical grounds. He left the Force two weeks later. He was given a good send off by his colleagues at Dereham.

Pegg went back to Pat's house in High Bradfield, where he stayed for several weeks. Fred was pleased to be reacquainted with the German Shepherd Zena. When Pat was back from work, they managed to get some short walks in on the nearby Peaks. Pat's research project proceeded a pace, and the universal app was soon ready to go into production.

The couple travelled back to Norfolk, where they spent the weekend together before she had to go back to High Bradfield and Sheffield University. They spent all their weekends together, alternating between South Yorkshire and Mid-Norfolk. Pegg was still waiting for the invitation to Buckingham Palace.

In the meantime he worked very hard at improving his fitness. The support of both Pat and Angie had ensured his mental wellbeing got back to normal as well. He spent many an hour thinking about what he would do next. He looked at his academic qualifications. As well as an NVQ in Investigation which would entitle him for membership of the Association of British Investigators (ABI). He could be a certified private investigator. He also had a HNC in Electrical Engineering. Perhaps he could study for a full blown degree in the subject. Food for thought. There were lots of things he could be doing post the Job.

Printed in Poland
by Amazon Fulfillment
Poland Sp. z o.o., Wrocław

62363127R00134